D1594286

The Write ONE

AUTHOR OF THE KISS ME CRAZY SERIES

JAMI ROGERS

To All The Romance Readers

Your passion for reading and sharing all things romance keeps me going.

Cover design © Hang Le byhangle.com

Editor: Julie Sturgeon, CEO Editor, ceoeditor.com

Proofreading: Owl Eyes Proof and Edits, www.owleyesproofsedits.com

Visit my website: www.authorjamirogers.com

❀ Created with Vellum

The Write ONE

AUTHOR OF THE KISS ME CRAZY SERIES

JAMI ROGERS

CHAPTER ONE

HERO

A cold beer, some sun, and good friends never hurt anyone.

Especially not today. It's a good buddy's birthday. The guys and I all finally have time to get together and relax. And just minutes before I got here, my agent let me know that the rumor in the publishing world is that I'm in the lead to receive the award for author of the year.

Author of the year.

God, I can't even think about it without grinning like a fool in love. I've wanted this since my first book hit the shelves a decade ago. Of course, I won't know for a couple more months if I've won. The winner is usually announced a week before the annual Lovers Convention. It's hosted by *Lovers Magazine,* or L-Mag as it's commonly known. They are *the* biggest company in the romance publishing world. If you want book talk or book gossip, L-Mag is where you want to be.

Their reviews have turned no-name authors into best sellers, and they've also tanked a career or two. Still, the Lovers Convention is the biggest reader and author event of the year. The first part is full of workshops for authors, and the last two days are one giant book fair for readers where they can buy books and meet their favorite authors. Pictures are taken, memories are made, and awards are given.

To me, hopefully.

I think it's safe to say that at this point, knowing I'm officially in the running to win, I'll do anything to seal that title.

"Hot damn, you did it again."

I chuckle, sipping my cold beer as my closest friend and one of my writing critique partners, Zane, clamps a hand on my shoulder.

"What a surprise," he goes on sarcastically. "I was worried that this book wasn't going to be a best seller. Were you worried?"

He's referring to my latest release. At this point in our lives, when doesn't he tease me about my books? If anyone hits the lists as often as I do, it's Zane. A little friendly competition is good.

I shake my head and point at my watch with the neck of my drink. "You're late."

He waves his hand between us. "That wasn't my fault."

"Oh yeah, and whose fault was that?"

He grins. "That would be the guest I had over for the afternoon. You know the tall, leggy, and—"

"Afternoon?" I ask, cutting him off and letting out a slow breath. "I have no idea how you do it."

My schedule has always been tight, and from what I know about my good friend, his is too. I've yet to manage balancing success and a love life. It really does amaze me how he does it so effortlessly.

"Um, I do. It's called I write romance. You should try it sometime, since, you know, you write romance too. You know every little move and action a woman craves. Put it to use in real life."

I don't judge Zane and his choices, but I just can't do what he does. I'm a one-woman kind of man. Well, I would be if I had a woman. Like I said, I'm busy. Potential award winner here, and I didn't get here by not working hard. If anything, I'm dating my deadlines.

"That's not my style and you know it."

He laughs. "That I do know. You're the deep POV writer of the group. The one who really tugs at the heartstrings." He clutches a hand to his chest to drive his point home. "The one who rips your heart out before they put it back together with just pages to go."

I can't help but smile. His interpretation of my writing style is both accurate and impressive.

"Oh, please. And what does that make you?" I ask.

"The slow burn."

I burst out with laughter as Zane leans down to grab a beer out of the cooler by our feet. I glance around at our friend Tobias's backyard and the people I've met in passing or don't know.

"Are the others coming?" Zane asks, nodding toward the house.

"Last I checked they were. They never miss Tobias's annual birthday BBQ, so you know they will be here, but they'll be late. It's the same for all of us these days: everyone has a busy schedule or deadlines to maintain. I still can't believe that Tobias decided to have this get-together. He's behind on a book that was due two weeks ago and has been submitting chapters by the day. He needs to have the last three turned in tonight."

Zane shakes his head. "I'd shit a brick if I even came close to a deadline. This is exactly why we plan. Then again, Tobias thrives off pressure."

"That he does."

I'll never forget the day I met Tobias. He'd been sitting

outside our creative writing class, his fingers speeding across his laptop right outside the door. We had a paper that was due as soon as we walked in the door, and he was still writing it. I was so appalled; I stopped to talk to him. Clearly, he didn't care about being done on time and yet, when he looked up at me with a grin and pulled a portable printer out of his bag, I couldn't help but admire his determination. I was sure we were polar opposites, but from that day forward, we started meeting up weekly to talk about writing. We were the first of our group. We truly thought we were just a random pair of guys who chose to write romance, but slowly, our group formed and now there are six of us.

"Do you know her?" Zane asks and points with his beer.

I glance over my shoulder at the blonde who just walked through the side gate.

"Nope."

"You'd think that after living here for as long as we have that we'd know more people."

I sip my beer, nodding. "That's the problem with being a writer. We get holed up in our houses for long periods of time."

"Are you sure you don't know her? You've lived here longer than I have."

It's a fact. Tobias and I are actually the only two of the group who actually grew up in Wind Valley, Wyoming. We lucked out that the college here had a badass English writing program. Plus, the college here has a direct link with the state university, so it was nice to get a degree without the big fancy school and sorority and fraternity distractions. Not to say that we didn't do our fair share of partying, because, boy, did we. It was a bit much at times, but it was nice to keep things low key for the most part. The others in the group followed suit after college and planted roots. It's the perfect place if you want the bar scene, an outdoorsy life, the city feel but still have peace and quiet. It's a one-of-a-kind place to live.

"Yep, I'm sure," I answer after one more look.

"Where is the birthday guy, anyway?" Zane asks, pulling out his phone and opening his text messaging app.

"Inside with Natalie, last I saw."

Zane groans. "Those two should just date already."

"Yeah, I'm pretty sure everyone sees it but them. Their time will come."

Knowing Tobias, he won't be the first to admit it. Really knowing him, he will wait until the day Natalie is at the church steps ready to say I do to some lucky man before Tobias figures it out. He'd wait for the last minute to feel the pressure.

"Oh, don't look now, but the birthday boy, his best friend, and *her* best friend are approaching."

Her best friend? Who is Natalie's best friend other than Tobias?

I turn around to look, then spin right back around.

Holy shit.

Nora Grayson is here.

Without moving a muscle, I look for any exit that will get me out of here before she spots me. Chances are, she already has, but we haven't made eye contact, so I might stand a chance.

My heart beats faster and my palms sweat.

Is she back for good? Just visiting? Why didn't anyone mention this to me?

"Are you okay?" Zane asks.

I nod but swallow back the dry lump in my throat.

Fuck. I don't have time for this.

"You could try harder at faking a smile," Zane says under his breath.

"This is the best you're going to—happy birthday, man," I recover quickly and clink my beer against Tobias's.

He hands both Zane and I another drink and smiles.

"I'm glad you guys could make it. Our schedules suck this year. How many books are you putting out, Zane?"

"Too many to count." He shakes it head. "I need to average about a book every six weeks to stay on track."

I let out a long breath. "I do not envy that deadline schedule."

My eyes glance briefly to Nora's. Like always, the piercing blue gaze that looks back at me hitches my breath. She squints and then looks away, taking a drink of her beverage. Water.

She would be the one to drink water at a party. Not that there's anything wrong with not drinking alcohol, but she always found a way to stand out.

"Hero, I can't believe you had another release this week. What is that? Four already this year and it's only the first week of June?" Natalie asks. She nudges Nora's arm.

"Yeah, way to go," Nora says deadpan.

Nora doesn't like me in the slightest. But as crazy as this is going to sound, well, Nora is what I call my unicorn. She's the girl I had the chance to be with and blew it. Like, I blew it before it even began. So now, when I'm around her, it's a mix of nerves and terror. Hence why I can't stop staring at her and also want to flee.

As far as I know, she's been living in LA for the last three maybe four years, so I haven't seen her much despite her family living here. Truthfully, I was certain the situation between us would change eventually, but it seems it hasn't.

I'm still stunned to silence by her eyes, by her long, strawberry blonde hair that shines under the sun, by the way she still smells like peaches, and how just being near her makes me feel like I'm running out of air. Don't even get me started on the fact that she's clearly traded in her signature maxi dress look for short spring dresses with white sneakers.

Once upon a time I was counting down the minutes until I saw her again, and then … I wasn't.

"Hero, did you hear me?" Natalie says, waving a hand in front of my face.

"Huh?"

"Your book, are you thrilled it hit the charts?"

"Oh, yes, of course."

"It's not like it's a surprise," Tobias says through a laugh. "Hero is an anomaly. He wrote one crazy love story and put it out for the world to read and it became a best seller within a week. Now, everything he writes just hits higher and higher on every list."

"Ooh, is someone jealous?" Zane asks.

"Hardly," Tobias says just as Beck walks up to the group.

Beck is our resident swoon writer. We all write what I'd like to think are swoon-worthy books, but no matter what kind of character he puts in his stories, I swear his readers swoon harder for him as a writer than for the people in the actual book. I've read a lot of his novels, and I won't lie, they are the words of a man searching for love if I have anything to say about it. I think his readers can feel it.

"Sorry I'm late," Graham, the clean romance writer of the group, says as he arrives. Simon "I write what I want when I want because I'm a single dad" comes up right behind him.

"My sitter ran late," Simon says.

And that's our group. Romances writers to the core, but all-around normal guys if you ask us.

"I plan for this party to go pretty late, so I wasn't worried," Tobias says. "Let's go grab a beer."

When Simon, Graham, and Tobias head toward the house, Nora grabs Natalie's arm. "I'm going to take off."

"No, why?" Natalie whines. "You just got here."

I turn my attention toward Zane, who is reading something on his phone, but I can still hear them loud and clear.

"I know, but I have work to get done, and I want to get ahead before the movers get here with the rest of my things on Monday."

So she's moving back?

"Fine. You're lucky we now have endless days to see each other."

"I do find myself pretty lucky," Nora says with a laugh that reminds me of the night I met her our sophomore year of college. I'd heard her laughing behind me at an off-campus party, and when I turned around and we locked eyes, I knew I'd never forget this girl.

And I haven't. Funny thing is, I'm sure she'd do anything to forget about me.

"Night," Nora says, leaving Natalie with Zane and me as she lets out a sigh.

"So, Nora's back in Wind Valley, huh?" I ask.

Natalie fights a smile as she stirs her blue drink. "She is."

"That's cool."

"It *is* cool." Natalie's face lights up. "I missed her, and I'm pretty excited to be working with her again."

"Oh, right. Tobias mentioned that she went off on her own a few months back. His online presence has been on fire since she started representing him. He's pretty pleased."

That's an understatement. All the guys, except me, use her for marketing. Last I heard, she had a waiting list for new clients.

Now, it helps that my friends and I all have the same agent, who oddly enough, is Nora's cousin. And to be fair, Doug has never asked me if I wanted to hire her. Honestly, I'm glad he hasn't, because I know she would say no. I'd rather never ask than have her turn me down.

"Holy shit," Zane says, his arms reaching toward me, but

flinging around as he grabs the attention of more people than I think he was intending to. "Holy shit!" His voice grows higher with each word.

"What's going—?"

"Get your phone out. Get your phone out!" he shouts.

Natalie and I share a confused look, but we both do as he says. Zane never gets this excited over anything. What he's about to tell us is either amazing news, like his latest series was just picked up by Netflix, or it's bad news that none of us want to hear.

As soon as I unlock my screen, my phone starts to ring.

"It's Doug." I show him my phone to justify why I can't join in on his reaction to whatever it is he has on his phone.

Zane looks at me with wide eyes.

"Dude, you aren't going to like this."

I don't have enough time to process the pity on his face before he's thrusting his phone at me.

"Hello," I greet my agent, but the next word hangs in limbo as I look at Zane's phone and read the review from *Lovers Magazine*.

There is no doubt about it, folks, Hero Quinn knows how to suck you in with a great romance. Yet, despite the well-crafted characters and vivid descriptions, I can't help but feel that the heat between the hero and heroine of his latest novel has fallen flat. It was as if a robot were controlling them. A robot that has never fooled around even once in its life. It's a hard pill to swallow, but perhaps this romance writer extraordinaire has lost his touch due to a lack of romance in his personal life. Dare I say that he's forgotten what it's like to be in love, or even lust? Better luck next time to this favorite author of mine.

What in the ever-loving hell is this?

CHAPTER TWO

NORA

Organization is key.

I cross my legs, placing my laptop on the computer table in my lap. My TV is directly behind me, so that I can hear the noise but not be distracted by the screen. On my left, I have two notebooks, one for each client I'm currently working on, and my row of colored highlighters is to my right. A different color holds a different purpose. Finally, I have three black fine point Pilot pens right next to the highlighters. It's going to be a late night, but I am going to cross task after task off my checklist as if I were eating Barbeque Baked Lays and watching *Bridgerton*.

Needless to say, I'm ready.

I wasn't always like this, but college was the eye-opener I needed. I always knew I wanted to work with marketing and social media. To have the ability to reach someone's mind so deeply that they follow you or buy a product fascinates me.

I'm twenty-nine years old and have won awards for my skill. I'm a very wanted woman, and because of this, I'm more than grateful that I've been able to work my job from any location in the world. It's a big reason why I chose to move back home to Wind Valley, Wyoming. LA was great, but it's busy and loud.

That's what's so perfect about Wind Valley. I get to work the big-city job and live in a not-so-big city town. It's not a small town by any means, but sixty thousand people give me a lot more breathing room than millions. Hiking trails are minutes away, a lake with one of the country's most elite lodges is just a couple hours away, and we get all four seasons. Five if you feel like giving the wind its own.

A warm early June breeze flows through my back door and over my face. I smile at nothing and let out a breath. It was nice being outside celebrating Tobias's birthday earlier. If I didn't have so much work, I would have stayed. I definitely chose the right time to move back. Had I come back in the midst of winter, I might be rethinking the whole thing.

I blow out another sigh. If only my patio furniture were here already.

How is it still this beautiful after the sun has gone down?

But this right here, the peace and calm, is what I love about Wind Valley.

I dive into work, scheduling out the next month for one client and creating a Facebook versus Instagram proposal for another. Really, though, both reach a different type of audience, and both would make a great choice. Yet this customer wants to use only one.

As soon as I'm finished with those, I grab another notebook and get to work.

The book tour season is about to begin, so my workload to make sure I keep authors' readers up-to-date is higher than normal.

I still can't believe I landed the Atlas deal. They are a major publishing house that was like finding the gold at the end of a rainbow. I'm honored that they picked me as their main marketing manager. It's a hefty workload, but I can handle it.

I'm still flipping through my notes when my phone rings.

It's almost ten, so there is only one person it could be. My assistant and best friend Natalie. They say you should never hire your friends, but this is the one case where that rule doesn't apply. If it weren't for Natalie, I wouldn't be where I am today.

She's probably calling to tell me what I missed at Tobias's BBQ. I could use the break.

"Hey, Natalie," I answer without even looking at my phone.

"Of course you're still awake."

"If you thought I was sleeping, why did you call?"

"Because I was just leaving Tobias's house and you missed something I thought might be of interest to you."

A smile touches my lips as I shake my head. Tobias is Natalie's other best friend. She met Tobias in college—he and his friends sparked the idea for what I should focus my career on, although to be fair, I never enjoyed hanging out with Tobias's friends much. One in particular I still don't care for, but the point is, Natalie and I were roommates, and she was always gushing about the books these guys wrote before they were even published and therefore suggested I look into specializing in the publishing industry.

Her idea had merit and here I am, working with writers in any genre.

"You called me at 10 p.m. to gossip?"

"Basically, yeah. It's about Hero."

I close my eyes and pinch the bridge between my eyes. Just hearing his name raises my body temperature. And not in a way that I want. I'm fully aware that I shouldn't still hold any type of emotions toward this guy—college was years ago—but it's hard. I thought I'd have a week or so to warm up to the idea that I'd see him around town eventually, but then he was in the backyard. Standing there all gorgeous as ever. Typically, I like a guy with a good buzz haircut, but Hero has grown his out a little. It's not long by any means, but it's definitely long enough to run my hands through it. God, and it looked softer than mine. I'm annoyed that I wanted to touch it. And the facial hair, ugh. I liked it.

I swear tonight was the first time I realized he had blond hair or that he was at least six feet tall. Then again, everyone is tall to my five-five height.

And the way he makes jeans and a simple black T-shirt look irritates me.

Hero is attractive. That's probably why I still get worked up at the thought of him. It's not fair to be cruel to someone the way he was to me and still be that good-looking. It's just not.

A part of me sort of hoped I'd get as lucky as I did growing up. You know, when Hero and I grew up in the same town, went to different schools but didn't meet till college. Guess I'm not that lucky this time around, because unlike my childhood, I'll be seeing him a lot. I blame Natalie. She just had to be besties with one of his friends.

"What about him?" I ask, getting back to the conversation. I really do have more work to do tonight. "And how is this of interest to me?"

"The L-Mag just gave him a bad review."

I take my glasses off and move my computer table off my lap. "What?"

"Yeah, you heard me. A bad, *bad* one."

"Send me the link."

I move my computer to my kitchen table because this is serious table work stuff. A bad review from *Lovers Magazine* is not the end of the world, but it's definitely not good.

I open my email and double-click the link.

"Holy shit, Natalie."

"I know. I feel bad for him."

"This is ..."

"Bad."

So bad. Everyone in our industry knows he's up for author of the year, and this review could keep him from that. Not that I care if he wins it or not.

Still, he needs a good spin on this. Something fast. If he has a girlfriend, now would be the time to announce it. Damn, I could get lost with ideas on how to fix this.

"It's being forwarded around nonstop. I even saw a meme already," Natalie says.

That's how famous Hero Quinn is in the writing and reading community. People love you when they love you, but they aren't afraid to take you down.

"I can't believe they just referenced his personal life like that. He could have a girlfriend."

Natalie laughs. "Please. That man is just as dedicated to his work as you are, if not more."

And that is the only redeemable trait, in my eyes, he has going for him.

He shouldn't be punished for that. No one should. But it isn't like I'm going to say that out loud to Natalie and defend him.

"Maybe when you see him in the morning at the coffee shop, you could say something to him. Check on him."

"Me?" I choke out. "Who says I'm going to see him tomorrow in the coffee shop?"

"I do because that's where you want to meet in the morning, and I have it on good word from Tobias that Hero goes to the coffee shop every Sunday morning to write. He needs a change of environment from time to time."

"Well, we share a favorite coffee shop. That's fine. But you know what we don't share? Conversation. Ever."

"You two used to talk all the time."

"No, we did not."

"Whenever the group was together, the two of you would talk."

"We'd argue. There's a difference."

"Well, still, it might be nice coming from you."

I let out a strangled noise, and Natalie sighs into the phone. "Will the grudge you two have for each other ever fade?"

"Unlikely."

"He stood you up on a date like seven years ago, Nora."

"So? He never once apologized, and the next time I saw him, he was making out with some other girl. He clearly has no respect for women."

Truth be told, I wasn't even mad at him for kissing someone else. I deserved better. I deserved an explanation. I didn't get either but instead of just moving on, I decided that hating him worked better than accepting that the one night we spent together, the night I swore we had a once-in-a-lifetime connection just before he asked me out, wasn't real. It's so stupid too. No girl should ever waste her time or energy on a man who clearly doesn't have enough respect for her to even send an "I'm not going to make it" text.

"So are you telling me you've never read one of his books?"

"No, I haven't. Why would I?"

That would be nothing but torture. Confirming that he clearly knows how to write a character who can treat a woman right but can't apply it to real life? Not for me anyway. No thanks.

"Nora, you do know he's known for writing a strong female lead, right? Like, there are even theories going around that it's really a woman who writes his books and said woman just uses Hero's face for a physical presence."

I had heard that, and I thought it was a joke.

"Doesn't matter. Hero made his impression on me, and he has yet to make a different one."

"Fine, okay. Moving on ..."

Natalie moves on to a new topic, but I don't hear her because the text that comes through captures my attention.

I groan.

"It's not that big of a deal. You could say no."

"What?"

"The wedding this weekend. You know, your brother and my sister. We are about to become real family to each other. Did you get your dress back already, or do you want me to pick it up for you this week?"

"Oh, yeah, yeah. I got it. I was groaning because James texted me *again*."

I really should have used a different Realtor when I was house hunting down here, but his family has the best reputation. I would have thought he'd have moved on from me by now. Shoot, I was gone for *years*.

"Oh no. You have to talk to him, Nora."

"I know. Just not yet. So how was the rest of the party?" I quickly change the subject.

Natalie fills me in on how laidback it was and how she's missed being around that group when they are together. She also fills me in on how Tobias was hanging out with everyone but stealing five minutes here and there to type at the laptop he had open at his kitchen island.

To each their own style, I guess.

We hang up, planning to meet up in the morning. With movers coming and cable guys, etc. this week, I don't really have any time other than Sunday to meet.

Which brings me back to the coffee shop in the morning. Will I mention something to Hero if I see him?

As a member of our shared industry, I feel for him. As a woman who desperately wants to move on from a man who made her fall for him one night only to break her heart the next, nope. I'll probably pretend I don't even see him.

CHAPTER THREE

HERO

His cock was huge.

It was so big that I could barely wrap my fingers aro—

"Wow. This is pure shit writing."

Twenty minutes and that's all I've written … and now deleted.

I jam the delete button until my computer screen is nothing but a blank white page. The same damn blank page that has been mocking me every day for the past few days. Sit down, stare at a blank screen, and repeat.

Today is no different.

I've written hundreds of sex scenes in my career and yet, today, my creative brain can't come up with anything other than the typical giant cock and groans and "yes, more. Do it again, harder" dialogue.

My editor is going to kill me. If I can't shake this feeling, I'm going to turn into Tobias, with Doug breathing down my neck. I've never missed a deadline, and although I still have more than a month, this could be a first for me.

I click out of the Word doc and back to the L-Mag's review

of my latest release, which I now have bookmarked on my computer. Talk about personal sabotage. Cringing, I scroll down to the review that started this entire downward spiral of not writing. I have the last few lines memorized at this point.

This brings a thought to mind and it's a hard pill to swallow, but perhaps this romance writer extraordinaire has lost his touch due to a lack of romance in his personal life. Dare I say that he's forgotten what it's like to be in love, if anything, in lust? Better luck next time to this favorite author of mine.

Fuck me.

I slam my laptop closed.

It doesn't matter that in the week since it's been released, I've had a few thousand reviews or ratings with a ninety percent five-star average.

Nope. No matter how many times I read that one critic, the annoyance and anger I feel doesn't lessen.

They didn't write a book. Do they even know what goes into a sex scene? The details. The edits. The rewrites. Where the hands go and when, how fast the hero or heroine moves their hips. Who's going to talk dirty and who isn't. That's not even all of it.

"Okay, time," Graham calls out, and the consistent clicking of keyboards that had filled my living room comes to a halt.

I look up.

Unlike me, my group of friends all have pleased smiles on their faces.

"You know, it's a good thing we're all used to your outbursts during these writing sprints." Zane doesn't even look up from his computer as he speaks. He's still typing away.

"Isn't that the truth? I almost lost focus when he slammed his computer, though." This coming from Beck.

"How many words did you get, Hero?" Tobias asks.

"Zero."

Simon shakes his head. "Don't tell me you were reading that review again."

I toss my hands up in the air.

"I just don't understand how that's the conclusion they came to. I mean, they could've written anything. 'Great love story but the sex was boring or not as steamy as his last'—anything else. They basically told the entire world I'm not getting laid."

Zane snickers, and Beck tries to hide his grin. The others just look at me with pity.

"At least they left a review."

Typical Graham, turning every negative situation into a positive one.

"Not to mention that you even finished a book and published it within the last year."

I nod at Simon, who has been suffering a mad case of writer's block too.

I know. I get it. I should still celebrate my accomplishments and not let some person I've never met ruin my success.

I can basically kiss author of the year goodbye.

Fuck.

I thought this book was my best yet. I need to focus on something else. Stat.

"Enough about me. Simon, did you get through that fight scene you wanted to finish today?"

Listening to my friends share that they are still on track with their goals might be just what I need to forget about this review.

"Sort of, I guess. Thank you for asking."

"What about you, Graham? The meet cute go all right?"

"It's brutal, but I've got something there worth editing."

"Good."

We go around the table, talking about strengths and weaknesses of the words we did, or rather didn't, write during our sprints today. We meet every Wednesday at 6 p.m. to share the scenes we want to write before the night is up, and then we do three twenty-minute sprints with twenty minutes breaks to discuss or help anyone with a scene they are stuck on. After our sessions, we make goals for the days we are on our own.

Typically, this is my most successful night of the week. It has been since we all met. It's a dream job, and we're all living it.

"Thanks again for letting us meet at your house, even though I'm sure you wanted to do anything but write tonight."

Beck slaps me on the shoulder as he passes me for the front door where the rest of the group has already stepped through. I hadn't even noticed that they all packed up to leave.

I guess we aren't going to keep this meeting going tonight. It's probably for the best. My mind isn't in the right place, anyway.

"My house is always available."

"Look, I know you're upset about that review, but you know you're a phenomenal writer. Try to move past it."

"And if I can't?"

I rub the back of my neck. I've never been this hung up on a review before. I don't really know how to navigate it.

"Prove them wrong."

"Sure. Yeah. Every writer's motivational dream is to write a book solely to prove a critic's review wrong."

He chuckles.

"At least think about something else long enough to enjoy Natalie's sister's wedding this weekend."

"I will."

I'm already banking on the vibe of the day to revive my romance writing ways.

"I'll see you at the wedding. And submit that damn proposal already. Your publisher can't sell books for you if you don't tell them what you're writing next."

He flips me his middle finger as he heads for his truck.

I close the door and retreat into my now-empty house.

Prove them wrong.

My schedule doesn't exactly have the timeline to just toss in another book into my writing schedule to serve this purpose, but I don't exactly see another option. I can't come this close to winning the biggest award in my industry just to lose it to one shitty review. There must be a way to redeem myself, and another book is by far the easiest choice.

I don't need a relationship or a merry-go-round of women at my door for sex in order to write a good book.

Do I?

CHAPTER FOUR

NORA

Begging is a form of flattery, right?

Like right now, my cousin is on the phone begging me to rescue his client.

"Come on, Nora. You're the best in the business and my author is one of the hottest male romance writers out there. Toss me a bone, I beg you."

I shake my head, even though he can't see it through the phone. "No can do, Doug. I don't have any openings. Not even for your hottest male writer."

"I didn't even tell you who it is yet." His voice drips with temptation. But no matter how much he tries to intrigue me, I'm no fool. I know his entire client list, and right now, his hottest writer is Hero Quinn. Which is more reason to be thrilled that my current workload doesn't have room for even one more. Not one.

Just thinking of him makes me lose focus. I don't care that I'm a grown women who should be able to control myself better than I do when it comes to Hero. Trust me, I know—I need to move on. Stat.

"Like I said, Doug, I don't have the space nor the time. Speaking of time, I have a Zoom call in about twenty minutes that I need to prepare for."

I'm already prepared, but I'll say anything to move on from this conversation.

"What do I have to do to free up some of your space?"

"Unfortunately, there isn't anything you can do. I'm a busy woman. You said it yourself. I'm the best in the business."

I'm not cocky—I'm confident.

"Yeah, but he really needs this. I'll even help Aunt Nessy bake the cookies this year at Christmas. I know how much you love watching her stick her unwashed fingers into the dough bowl and eat it like it's frosting."

Damn. That's temping. I could definitely go without that visual this year.

"I'll tell you what, if someone cancels on me—and we both know they won't— you can have first dibs on my availability."

"That's the best you can do?"

"Doug, would you talk to another possible marketing company this way?"

"No."

"Then stop sounding like I drove over your bike. Yes, that is the best I can do."

"Fine." His sigh is a dead giveaway that he isn't finished. "Are we still on for dinner this Sunday? If I don't show up this week, your mom will kill me. Mine too. Sisters can be crazy."

"Well, you're my only cousin who continues to skip out."

"I live six hours away. It's not a drop-in family gathering for me like it is for the rest of you. I have to plan my whole weekend."

"Well then, you better get to planning. I need to get back to work."

"Fine. Tell your mom I said hello."

"Will do."

As soon as the call ends, I adjust my seat closer to my computer and focus on this month's schedule. The rumors that have been going around about Atlas closing their publishing doors have been brutal, but I assume it's all false since they contracted me out for the next year.

I spend the next few minutes preparing for the Zoom call with Alan, the Atlas rep, and even log into the meeting ten minutes early.

Except, those ten minutes go by too quickly. Ten becomes fifteen and fifteen becomes twenty. Leaving the meeting open, I send Alan an email.

It bounces back almost immediately.

That's odd.

I send another.

Same thing.

I dial the number listed on the last email I received from him, and it doesn't waste any time giving me the "this number has been disconnected" auto response.

I slowly lower my cell.

No.

No.

No.

I click into Internet Explorer and search Atlas Publishing.

The articles that pop up turn my stomach over immediately.

I skim quickly, my brain both processing what I'm reading but also trying to decide if my eyes are playing tricks on me. Maybe it's time I get my eyes checked.

However, today is not that day. I am, in fact, reading this time.

Atlas, the company I was just mentally raving about, is indeed going out of business. And if they are going out of business, then I can guarantee the contract we signed is null and void.

I'm out of work.

I lean back on the couch and stare at the television screen. How am I going to replace that income? It's going to take multiple jobs to come close. What's more, I had to turn job after job down just to take this deal, so I don't have enough opportunities just waiting for me. Those authors have surely found someone by now.

Shit.

This blows. Atlas has been thriving for decades. I grew up reading book after book from them.

I let out a deep breath and then shut my computer. I won't be able to focus now.

Tomorrow will be better. I'm going to my brother's wedding, after all. Nothing can be bad about that.

CHAPTER FIVE

NORA

I like weddings, but right now, I'm sweating like a sinner sitting in the first pew at church.

One. Two. Three. Look.

I peek through the small window of the kitchen door, scan the reception hall, and resume my hiding position.

“It is such a waste to hide that gorgeous dress in a banquet hall kitchen.” Sherrie tsks and crosses something off the clipboard in her hands.

“Perks of going to the same school as the wedding planner?”

I haven't seen Sherrie in years, but right now I’m sure thankful for all those gym classes we’d skip to go get coffee.

“You should be out there with your brother. Not in here with me.”

“And I would be if James weren’t here.”

“You’re a grown woman, Nora. Plus, I’m sure that by now he knows you two are completely broken up and not getting back together.”

I pull out my phone from my clutch and shove the screen in her face.

"I'm so excited to see you tonight. I miss you. Let's talk." She cringes and her face makes the replica of mine earlier when I spotted my ex during the ceremony.

Ugh.

Every time I looked into the crowd, my eyes found his as if he'd been sounding a foghorn, forcing me to look in his direction. I can't believe I forgot that Natalie's sister is friends with him. That's how I'd met James. Natalie had her sister set us up, and I went because I hadn't dated anyone since Hero had stood me up. Then I kept seeing James because … why not? I had no idea what I was getting myself into.

Damn it.

I'm surprised I haven't puked from nervousness. I've been known to get sick in these moments.

"Maybe he just needs closure. I mean, until today, the last time he saw you, he was down on one knee, watching you run to the nearest bathroom to fake diarrhea."

I gasp.

"I. Was. Shocked. Anyone can get an upset stomach from nerves. And a marriage proposal after six months fully warrants a gut full of diarrhea."

A waiter steps into the kitchen just as the last few words fall off my lips.

He basically leaps away from me.

"Not right now. It was … never mind. Why am I explaining myself?"

"All right, well, not only did you run off to the bathroom, but you also moved to a whole new state the next week. Care to explain that one?" Sherrie asks.

"Easy. I got a job offer I couldn't refuse."

And that is the god's honest truth right there. Now, could I have handled the proposal better? Yes. Was taking the job my easy out? Also, yes. I was fresh out of college. My choices, although not regrettable, weren't always the right ones. And yes, I learned the hard way. It's a big reason why I'm back in Wyoming. I miss the person I am when I'm here.

Sherrie rolls her eyes. "You're an adult, Nora. Just tell him the truth so you can both move on. You need to go out there."

Tell him the truth. I have. It's over. How much clearer can I be?

I let out a deep breath. No matter how long I stand here to justify why I shouldn't go back out there, she's right. Tonight isn't about me.

"If you see me out there talking to James, bring me something uncooked. I'll need a really good exit strategy."

She shakes her head with a laugh. "You're ridiculous."

I barely hear her as I push through the door.

Here I go. To the reception, I mean. Who cares how old I am? I have zero intentions of confronting James. Some people just don't handle those situations well. Me. I'm those people.

A quick scan shows no signs of my ex, but it does pass Hero, directly in front of me. Dear lord, that man is a sin sent straight from heaven. I'm not even being cheesy or exaggerating. If Thor and Wonder Woman—the Chris Hemsworth and Gal Gadot versions—had a daughter and Kate Beckinsale and Tom Hardy had a son and those babies had a child, that would be Hero. Specifically, Hero in a tux.

All the more reason for me to despise him. It should be illegal to be that good-looking and an ass. Yes, I said ass. If I relate Hero to anger, I'm more likely to forget about any other version of him. Which, let's be honest, is a pretty great goal to have now that I've moved back.

Oh, damn. Here he comes.

"Nora," Hero says and points across the room. I grab his hand as he says, "Isn't that—?"

"Ahhh!" I lunge to cover his mouth with my hand, thankful for my quiet wedge heels at this moment, and look around us.

The coast is clear.

Slowly, I remove my hand and whisper, "Don't say a word, and for the love of all things holy, do not point."

"Why not?"

I almost laugh when he whispers back.

"Certain people don't need to be informed of where I am in this room at this very moment."

"Like whom?"

"Like certain people."

He doesn't need to hear my drama.

"Your secret is safe with me." He nods once and winks.

Good-looking and cruel, Nora.

"You look beautiful tonight. That color is really becoming on you."

"Thanks," I manage to say as if I'm not affected. Which I'm not. I'm only still standing here saving face because this is my brother's wedding, and I will not cause a scene on his big day. And talking to anyone, even Hero, means not talking to James.

"Nora!"

My attention jerks to my right as James shouts my name and waves, making a straight line for me.

"Shit," I say through a whisper.

"Problem?" Hero asks.

"Slight."

"Your ex?"

I nod. "You come up with stories for a living. Any ideas on how to solve my issue? He's about to be here in three, two …"

"I've been looking for you all night," James says, and I swear he breathes as if he's just sprinted across the room.

"Hey, James. How are you?"

"Better now. Can we go somewhere and talk?"

I was so close.

I'm about to excuse myself and get this reunion over with, but Hero's hand rests on my right hip.

"We were actually about to head onto the dance floor, and if we know Nora, I better take the chance while I can, right, babe?"

Babe?

Hero's gaze captures mine, and he winks. I don't say anything, and he leans in, kisses my cheek and whispers, "Just go with it."

"Rain check?" I ask over my shoulder as Hero leads me to the dance floor.

James crosses his arms and glares as he watches us.

Hero pulls my body against his, one hand at my hip and the other in my hand.

"I have a proposal for you," he says quietly as we sway to the soft music.

"Of course you do." I should have known that his help would come with strings. "What is it?"

"I need to create the illusion that I'm in a relationship, and clearly so do you. I think we should do that with each other."

I laugh. "Or you could go get a real girlfriend, and I could take the grown-up route and once again, tell James it's over and he needs to move on."

"That's exactly why you are the perfect woman for this. You're blunt and no-nonsense. That's what I need."

"Are you telling me you've never written a pretend dating novel? Fake relationships are too complicated, and everyone ends up in love in the end."

"Well, yeah, but I think our current relationship will make that easier for us. You don't care for me, and I tolerate you, so I have high expectations that we won't be falling in love."

He tolerates me. *Please.*

"Still, I think it's a horrible plan. You'll have to find your Juliet with someone else."

"Come on, Nora, I just saved your butt back there, and you know it."

"What I know is that although I'm slightly, possibly grateful for the interference, had you not been there, I would have had to talk to my ex like an adult and clear the air."

"Which is?"

"That we are over and not getting back together and he clearly can't take the hint."

"You know," Hero starts. I roll my eyes. "You told your ex no and he keeps coming back, so either you suck at saying no or this guy sees something in you that I have yet to notice."

"I'm very clear when I say no."

"Sure."

The song ends, and so I step out of Hero's hold.

"Sorry I can't be the woman you're looking for. Better luck on the next one."

"Nora, come on. Please," he says as I walk away.

I pause and glance over my shoulder. "No."

He tosses his head back and laughs. That deep sound sends a flutter to my stomach, which sends a message to my brain, which likes hearing his deep, throaty laugh.

I hightail it out of there.

CHAPTER SIX

HERO

I can't believe I let Doug talk me into coming with him to a family barbeque. One they are clearly having the day after a wedding to entertain family members who haven't gone home yet. The only other outsider present is Natalie, but even she has a tie as the groom's sister.

"Do you normally take your contracted writers to family events?" I wave to who I think is his aunt—she works at the floral shop closest to my house, and then tuck my hands in my pockets. I should leave.

"Typically, no. But since you live in the same town as my cousin and we need her to take you on as a client, I need you two to hit it off. Oh, there's my mom. I better say hello to her before she flips a gasket."

I've tried to tell him more than once that Nora is unlikely to help me, even in a professional way, but Doug is persistent.

He rushes off to an older woman with red hair. She's definitely his mother. Their noses are like a cut and paste of each other.

"What are you doing here?"

The displeased tone behind me piques my attention. I sip my beer and keep my ears open. Doug wouldn't know if I added his family gossip to a book, would he?

"I'm talking to you."

Whoever this woman is talking to is in for it. She sounds pissed. I'm gathering that her tone is the exact reason this other person hasn't replied.

"Hero, I'm talking to you."

Oh shit.

I know that voice. I know it too well.

Nora.

I spin around, her ice-blue eyes boring into mine. She's not thrilled to see me.

I knew I would see her here. There is a point to me being here, after all, but I thought I'd have more of a heads-up. Like I would see her from across the room and could gather myself to figure out what to say. After the moment we shared at the reception last night when we didn't fight, I'd thought we were turning over a new leaf.

It seems I was wrong.

When it comes to Nora, I'm way out of my league. A league I fucking write for a living. And yet, she still turned me down at the wedding yesterday. If I were writing this story, the events of the wedding would have led to a deal for my hero and heroine. But this is Nora. Unpredictable Nora.

"Doug invited me."

She crosses her arms at her chest and shakes her head. "I'm sure he did. This is some ploy to get me to work for you, isn't it?"

I glance around the space, wishing that Doug would appear any moment.

"It wasn't my idea." Honesty is always the way to go, right?

She tosses her hands up and groans. "Unbelievable. I told

him no on the phone. I'm not working for you. You can fix whatever image damage control you need on your own."

I put a hand up. "He already asked you?"

"Yes, and I said no."

I put my hands on my hips and drop my chin to my chest. Damn it. This isn't a play nice and maybe she will say yes.

Joke's on Doug because there is literally nothing in this world that could get Nora to change her mind.

"I'll go talk to him."

"No, I'll do it." She walks past me.

I fall into step with her.

"Clearly, you saying no the first time didn't work."

"I'll be clearer this time."

"I'm not sure how much clearer *no* can be."

"I guess we are about to find out, aren't we?"

"Nora, stop," I call out and grab her arm. She glances down at my hand, and the look she gives me is like a wolf ready to gnaw his leg out of a trap. I pull it back.

"You don't need to talk to Doug."

"Clearly, I do." She folds her arms again as she studies me. "Why would you stop me?"

"Because if you don't want to work on my team, I don't want you on it."

She lifts her chin as if she's about to say something sassy, but she only nods.

"So, you'll tell him to stop asking me?"

I nod. "I will."

"Finally, something we can agree on."

"Right. I mean, it's not like you could have handled the work anyway."

She'd actually be the best for the job, but I'm not going to tell her that.

She huffs. "Typical."

"What?"

"You. Attempting this whole 'you'd suck at it' conversation to which I'll say 'no, I'd be the best,' and you taunt me to prove it and boom! I'm working for you. Just the way you planned all along."

"Do I really do that when I talk?"

"Do you do what?" She crosses her arms and glares at me. It's clear she is annoyed with me.

"That whole puff my chest out and pucker my lips thing that you just did when you were impersonating me. Is that what I look like?"

God, I hope not.

Her eyes narrow, and a sly smile touches her lips. "Yes, you do."

Her hands are on her hips now, and the fury in her eyes holds a familiar shimmer.

I just sip my drink and hold her gaze.

"Am I right?" She all but stomps.

"Is that how you talk to all potential clients?"

"You are not a potential client, Hero. Not now and not ever."

"Sure." I sip my drink.

"You do, except you also do this nervous tic thing with your hand. It reminds me of someone who is in recovery from a drug addiction."

My gaze falls immediately to my hands. What is she talking about? No one has ever mentioned this to me. Do I really? How would I even—?

Her laughter surrounds me.

"You're terrible," I say, taking yet another sip of my drink to hide my smile.

This is by far one of the best conversations I've had with Nora. We are going two for two on civil chats this weekend. I'm not opposed to it. Perhaps this little feud between us is coming to an end after all.

"I'm hilarious," she says and then walks away. "Good luck with your reputation, Hero."

I watch as she strides away, her hips swaying softly as she goes. I may not have been successful in getting her to agree to represent me, but when I get home, I write more words than I have in the past week.

That's progress, and it's progress I will take.

The next morning, however, I feel like everything has backtracked on me, and the voicemail from Doug doesn't help.

"Hero, we have a problem. Sales have plummeted, and if we want to lock that award into your name, we need a redemption. Let's chat soon."

Fuck.

CHAPTER SEVEN

NORA

Waking up early to get a jump on the day was a smart idea for this Monday morning. I have a long checklist. Finding more clients by returning calls and reaching out to a few authors I recently turned down is at the top of the list. Other action items include finishing my July calendar of preplanned postings for current clients and arranging newsletter features a few months out.

Traveling isn't part of my job, but I like to go above and beyond when I can. Plus, being a reader myself doesn't hurt. I support my clients in as many ways as possible. So I need to travel to the bigger signing conferences to get current data for social media accounts. I do more than social media, but right now, they are hot, and consistency is key. That brings me to another piece of my checklist: travel arrangements.

"Your focused face scares me sometimes," Natalie says, bringing me out of the trance I am in. Mentally repeating my checklist doesn't cross the items off any faster.

"Well, good." I'm not sure how to respond to that, but maybe it should scare her.

"Good?" she laughs. "How is that good?"

I shrug. "It's motivating?"

Her laughter is contagious. "You clearly need a break."

"I can't take a break, Natalie. I have simple tasks that need to be done but are taking forever."

"Well, let's look at the list and do the most productive first."

"No, let's do the easiest first."

She shakes her head. "No way. Do you remember that mindset podcast you made me listen to last year? Crossing off the most productive item first will relieve stress and free up time. So, what is that item on your list?"

Damn. She's right.

"Grow my client list since the Atlas deal is no more."

It's official. I was relieved of my contract over the weekend.

Next time, no matter who it is or how big the company, I will read the fine print.

"What are you doing to complete this? I sent you a list of potential authors who have inquired in the past."

I nod. "I reviewed it last night. Only three reached out within the last month, and I've made calls. I was able to forward a proposal to two of them, but the other one already found someone else."

"What's your next plan?"

"Find another big name to work with. Writer or publishing house—it doesn't matter to me."

"Well, duh. How?"

"I'm not sure."

"You could call your cousin."

I make a gagging noise. "So he can tell me to represent Hero. No thanks."

Trust me. I've thought about it more times in the last twenty-four hours than I want to admit. Representing him makes sense, but I just can't bring myself to do it. I sat in that restaurant all those years ago for more than an hour waiting for him. Sure, any girl would have left long before that, but I was so excited for our date that I waited. I even convinced myself that something bad happened to him.

I sigh. To be honest, seeing him this past week has left me conflicted. He seems to have grown up, which is great, but I haven't forgotten how he hurt me. It's not an easy feeling to let go of, and I don't want to open it back up. If I fall for him the way I did back then, I might not recover this time.

"It was fun to see you two at the wedding," Natalie says, blowing on her coffee and glancing over the top of the cup to look at me.

"Why do I get the sense there is more to that statement?"

She sets her cup down. "I mean, if you wanted to fill me in on how you ended up on the dance floor with Hero and yet are still opposed to working with him, I'm all ears."

Oh. That.

"Oddly enough, he was saving me from a one-on-one moment with James."

She gasps dramatically and puts her hand over her heart. "Hero Quinn swooping in and acting like a … hero?"

"Stop, stop." I put my attention back to my computer. "It was harmless."

"Sure it was. Is he a good dancer?"

He was actually pretty good. I don't have a lot to compare him to, but he was smooth with his movements, and when I close my eyes, I still feel the touch of his hand on my hip.

"He was okay."

"Tobias was telling me that your cousin reached out to you to help Hero's image more than once."

"He did." I never look up from my screen. "Haven't we already established this?"

She nods. "Ugh, yes, but why don't you take it? Adding him

to your list of clients wouldn't hurt. It's basically what you need to do."

"Working with him on the daily or even weekly would kill me."

"Come on, Nora. You know that if he even wants to stand a chance after that review, he needs you."

"As a matter-of-fact, I do know that, but this is not my problem."

Natalie is about to answer when the man himself walks through the door, Tobias and Zane trailing in after him.

"Ladies," Tobias says, ruffling Natalie's hair as he passes our table.

"Seriously." She swats at him. "I just did my hair."

Tobias laughs and follows Hero and Zane to the counter so that they can order their drinks.

"Should we ask them to sit with us?" Natalie whispers.

"Why would we do that?"

"Um, because they are our friends."

"That's a bit of a stretch, right?"

"Nora, come on."

I groan and move my computer so that they have room. They've all got their computers with them, so I'm sure this isn't just a casual meet-up.

"I would say that I'm surprised to see you here this morning, but I'm not," Hero says, taking a seat next to me since Tobias has already taken dibs on the one next to Natalie. He leans into her ear, whispers, and she erupts into laughter.

Those two. I swear, one day they will figure it out.

"What's that supposed to mean?" I ask with a bit more flare than I intended.

Our gazes hold for a split moment before he looks to the others. "Is this a joke?" he asks.

I lean back and cross my arms.

"If it is," Tobias says, "I'm lost but intrigued."

Hero sighs. "In college, it was Nora's MO to go to a coffee shop every single morning to get work done."

How does he know that?

I study him for a moment, but the comment doesn't seem to alarm him the way it does me.

"I hadn't realized anyone noticed," I say.

My statement catches him by surprise. He glances up. Everyone is looking at him.

His shoulders barely rise with a shrug. "You were pretty predictable back then."

I'm sure.

I shake my head and get back to work until my cell buzzes against the table. James's name appears. I silence the call and meet Natalie's eyes over my computer screen. Since we both work off Macs, her message comes through almost instantly to my screen.

Natalie: He's still calling you? Didn't you tell him it was over?

Nora: Multiple times.

Natalie: I wonder what his deal is.

Nora: If I knew, I'd remedy it and call it done.

Natalie: Maybe you need a vacation.

Nora: I wish. Oh, great, another pitch from Doug just came through. This man never gives up.

Natalie: What's the offer?

Nora: He wants me to show up to more book signings than originally planned.

Natalie: Do it. Space from James will be nice.

Nora: I like the way you think.

Natalie: And if you pick up Hero, the extra distraction will be nice.

She has a point.

Natalie: Let's say you choose to represent him. How can you fix this for him?

Nora: Not sure. It should be easy. I mean, look at him. What girl wouldn't want to date him? If there were an ad out there with his picture on it, girls would come flocking, and I wouldn't have to—oh my god, that's it! I'm going to set him up on dates. It's brilliant.

Natalie: Oh, no, you've got that look.

Nora: You bet your ass I do.

If I want to get over Hero Quinn once and for all, there is one sure way to do it. Find him a girlfriend.

CHAPTER EIGHT

HERO

Despite the sales drop, this week was going pretty well. I wrote some words I'm happy with in my current manuscript, I ran into Nora at the coffee shop and she didn't act like I was the devil himself—could have helped that our friends were there to be buffers—and I spent time with my sister, Sydney, while she, her husband, and my baby niece Stella were in town.

Like I said, sales dropping isn't the end of the world, and eventually it will pass, so all in all, it's been a pretty decent week. Until right now.

I'm going to go apeshit on Nora Grayson. As soon as I get off the phone with my agent.

"I'm sorry, Doug, could you repeat that?" The words are slow and steady, but on the inside, I'm screaming them.

His chuckle makes me wish I could reach through the phone, grip his shirt, and shake him. The last time I spoke with Nora, she was dead set against helping me. Practically laughed in my face at the mere idea of working together. But now … now she does this?

"We're going to set you up on a few blind dates with readers and document it. Show your fans that you're actively looking for love."

Lie. Lying to my fans is another way to put it.

"I'm not, though. It would be a joke."

"Come on, Hero. Everyone is looking for love. Who knows, maybe you'll find it over your two-week tour. You just never know when it might stick."

No, I like to shut my brain off on these tours. I like to take a break. Let my body relax so that I can go full steam ahead when I get home, and if I'm out galivanting around on blind dates because my new marketing manager thinks this is a great way to put myself out there, I'm not recharging. I'm about to spend two weeks on and off on book signings and meet and greets. Nora has clearly lost her mind in thinking I'll go through with this.

"I think we can think of something better."

Instead of pulling out my hair, I take a seat in my home office chair and grab a pen and notebook. *Think, Hero. Think.*

A survey to find love? Fuck. That's a brilliant idea for a story but a horrible idea for my real life.

I'm not doing it. She's mad.

So much for this truce I thought we were forming.

Damn, if anything, I officially know how much Nora does not like me.

"No way," Doug says quickly. "This is it. We are doing this. Look, Hero, I know it's not typical for your brand, but I think that is what makes it so genius. You write all these love stories and have yet to have one of your own. Ninety percent of your following are women. This is a smart move. It would be quite the story if you actually meet someone too."

"Highly unlikely." I pinch the spot between my eyes. This cannot be happening.

"It's like you say in your books: love is always unexpected. Not to mention that this so-called search for love could be just what you need to secure author of the year. Your books, despite recent reviews, are amazing. But damn, this would really show your dedication to the craft. Plus, I didn't want to tell you this, but there has been mention of bumping your name from the author of the year list."

"Are you kidding me?"

Oh god. I'm going to be sick.

"It's hasn't happened yet. Just rumors. I think this would help secure your spot. Show the L-Mag how much you value their opinion and are willing to make changes in order to provide the best books out there."

Damn it. The award. I've been so distracted lately, I almost forgot about it.

Fuck!

A survey, for crying out loud. A *survey*! She may as well have put an ad in the local paper.

Survey.

No matter how many times I say that word, I still don't like it.

This is just ridiculous.

"Do I get any say in this?" I ask. "Dating is not the same thing as writing new books. You do realize that, right?"

He sighs. "Yes, and yes, you get the final say. You could pull this whole entire thing right now, but I know that you know this will be great for your career all around. Two weeks. You can handle two weeks of sharing your love life. Plus, we both know Nora is a goddess at her job. She wouldn't ever steer us in a direction that would potentially make her look bad."

He's got me there.

Two weeks. That's it. When it doesn't work out, then what? What will my reputation be then? Pitied romance writer who couldn't find love?

At the same time, if I go in full steam ahead for two weeks, this whole disaster review and reputation thing will be behind me, and I can relax.

Two weeks.

Fourteen days.

Half a month.

Shit. Am I really going to do this? I mean, I don't have to give a rose or something fancy. I don't even have to communicate with these women outside of the date. Maybe I can get some good ideas for another book.

I groan loud enough for Doug to hear.

"Sounds thrilling."

"Sounds like you're not saying no. Plus, on the bright side, it's like six, maybe seven dates, max, out of the entire tour."

I close my eyes, rubbing my forehead. My life was great two weeks ago. I was on track for everything I wanted, and now, I'm about to date a bunch of women who were selected for me because of a goddamn survey.

Why would Nora do this to me?

"Any questions you might have, let me know, and I'll pass them to Nora."

You can bet your ass I'll have follow-up questions.

I can't believe I'm doing this.

"Well, if we are doing this, we aren't half-assing it. I want Nora along on the tour. I want her documenting every little thing. I want to know that this is a top priority for her. If we don't go at this 100 percent, it'll fall flat and chance the opposite effect."

"Nora. Tour. Full ass. Got it." Given the way he shortens it, I know he's writing it down. "I think she was planning to make an appearance anyway because a lot of my writers are her clients, too, but I'll let her know she needs to be in full attendance. I'll send her your itinerary and travel information so that she can line things up with yours. Do you want to call her, or do you want me to do it?"

Oh, I'd give anything to hear her response, but if I know one thing about Nora, it's that she has no problem telling me no.

"You can tell her. Thanks, Doug. See you in Chicago next week."

"See you next week."

* * *

I didn't expect to hear from Nora so soon after I spoke with Doug, but she called me within the hour and asked—well, pretty much informed me—that I needed to be at the coffee shop, pronto. I didn't bother asking which one.

So here we are, sitting across from one another with forced smiles. Alone. So, you know, expect the unexpected.

"I'm surprised you called me," I start the conversation, leaning back into the seat across from Nora. Her hair is in a messy bun, she's wearing a pink shirt that reads Just One More Chapter and ripped jeans with white sneakers. She looks beautiful, as always. A part of me wishes her looks would fade, but time is on her side more than it is mine.

"Well, I feel the tiniest bit sorry for not coming to you first." She pinches her index finger and thumb together and scrunches her nose.

"Just a tiny bit?"

She nods. "Yeah. I mean, you did come to me with the idea to trick readers into thinking you had a girlfriend. Lying, as I like to call it, is a smooth way to end your career. At least this way, even if the survey doesn't work out, your readers get to see you making an effort."

I nod slowly. She has a point, but still …

"Since I'm not actually looking for someone to date, I think this still counts as lying."

She flops a giant notebook open and shakes her head.

"No, but this is you making an effort, and besides, you might fall in love. In fact, I think you should try."

The girl who got away is telling me to fall in love with someone else. Heck if that isn't the best line I've thought of lately. My luck really is going downhill.

"But a survey, Nora? Was that really all you could come up with?"

"It's edgy and original. It's going to be a hit."

She starts to scribble away at something in front of her. I've been here five minutes, and I can already see that when she puts her mind to something, she's all in.

I'd push more, but damn, she does marketing wonders for the other guys. I have to trust her.

I run a hand through my hair and sigh.

"All right, so what are the questions you have in mind for these readers?"

They better be solid ones. Smart ones. Nothing like my favorite ice cream or any other food.

"Well," she tucks a stray piece of hair behind her ear, "so far, I have a mix of completing the answer, multiple choice, and place these in order lists."

A variety is a good start.

"Let's hear them."

"First, I have some general questions for you. At what age is too young for you?"

I narrow my gaze at her. "Is this a serious question?"

"Yes."

"Nora, come on."

"What? Is it just the legal age, or do you prefer older women? I have no clue."

"Let's go with twenty-seven."

"Really? Twenty-seven. That seems so specific."

"Next question."

She nods. "Right. Okay, I ask them to list three hobbies from favorite to least favorite. Regarding a night out, I like to fill in the blank: cats versus dogs, do you like kids, are you single, what's your ideal date activity, what is your favorite Hero Quinn book, and—"

"This is all over the place," I cut in. "I think we need to narrow this down."

"I'm trying to make this fun. It's not like I'm going to ask them how many kids they want or where they plan to settle down."

"Well, at least those questions would sound like I'm serious about this."

"You're right. I should add those in there."

"Do not do that."

Nora groans, covering her face with her hands.

"Trust me on this, okay?"

"To make me look like a fool, got it."

Her entire body perks up, and she immediately takes a deep breath, letting it out slowly.

"It's clear we do not get along. I understand that. I know I'm not kind to you or chatty when I'm in your presence, but let me get one thing straight with you, Hero. When it comes to my job, I am 100 percent perfectly focused. I give it my all, and I'm damn good at it. If I thought for one second that this idea would end up making anyone look like a fool, I would pull the idea in a heartbeat. The last thing my company needs is a bad review or reputation. You, of all people, should understand that."

I pinch my lips together. Well, hot damn. Nora is fierce, and I'm into it. This no bullshit approach works for me. She means business, and I won't tell her this, but her little speech to put me in my place just now worked.

I trust her.

She goes on: "Now, can we get back to the task at hand? We

have two days to finalize this before we go, and I do not want to waste any more time. My time, as I'm sure yours is, is valuable to me."

I nod, rubbing my chin to contain the smile itching to spread across my face.

"Great, thank you. I still can't believe I'm going with you. Two weeks for a book tour is crazy."

"It's only four stops all together." She's not wrong per se, but it's all about how you look at it. "Less than forty-eight hours for the first stop, then we stay longer at the others because we sign at multiple locations. All bookstores because I'm old school like that. Plus there are a few days off in between. It's really not that bad."

"I think six dates is a good number then, don't you?"

Six dates and they think I'll fall in love. She's crazy, but I'm supposed to trust her, right?

"Six dates it is."

"Good, now out of the questions I asked you, which ones do you want to use?"

I spend the next forty-five minutes making all the final details with Nora.

The idea of a survey still makes me uneasy, but I did learn something today. Nora is confident, smart, driven, and she takes no shit from anyone. Me included.

CHAPTER NINE
HERO

I prefer flying over driving.

In fact, I fly so much that I have perfected how to pack for two weeks in a carry-on bag. Tip number one, book hotels that offer complimentary overnight laundry services.

The line for security isn't long by any means, but I still look over my shoulder for Nora.

She's nowhere in sight.

If she isn't on this plane, bets are, she's already in Chicago.

We didn't discuss flights. Well, not with each other. I talked to Doug, and she talked to Doug. That man goes above and beyond typical agent duties without complaining. Taking a chance on him right out of college was the best choice I ever made.

As soon as my belt is back in place, I find a place near the gate. The Wind Valley airport has only four gates. Everything is easy to find.

The moment I sit, my phone starts to beep obsessively.

I open the app with the most notifications.

My face is the first thing to pop up.

Win a date with Hero Quinn!

I stare at the words typed under the photo and fidget in my seat.

Complete this survey and match up as many answers as you can with our "hero," and you just might win yourself a date with him. He's on tour for the next two weeks, so now's your opportunity. Just click here and take a chance on love.

Oh dear god.

I quickly pull up my email, ready to send my thoughts to Nora, but my thumb hovers.

No. I've got this. Nora's got this.

Trust her.

I go back to the apps. Since Nora's company tagged me in the post, I should share it, right? With a comment.

Hey, ladies ...

Gross.

One lucky lady ...

Delete. Delete. Delete.

Maybe I shouldn't write a comment. Maybe I should type an emoji and a hashtag and then post it.

No.

Shit, why is this so hard?

Ping.

Ping.

Before I can make a decision, my phone begins to go off again, but these are text messages.

Ping.

Ping.

What the heck?

Ping.

Ping.

Ping.

I jam my finger on the volume button until it's completely

silent. The sounds might be gone, but the number in the red bubble over my messenger app is counting.

Do I really want to look and how is this possible? It's been like sixty seconds.

Zane: Hahahahaha DUDE!

Tobias: Social Media! That's how you tell us!

Simon: I thought we were closer than that.

Graham: I didn't realize you were looking for someone.

Zane: I just scolded him in another text for not telling us first.

Beck: For not telling us what? I'm lost.

Tobias: Check your Instagram, Beck.

Hero: How have you all already seen it? It was just posted.

Beck: What picture? My phone won't load anything. What am I missing?

Zane: I get notifications on all the posts this group makes. I like to be supportive, and I don't want to miss a thing.

Tobias: Same.

Graham: Ditto.

Simon: *nodding gif*

Beck: I just saw it. Now you guys are making me feel like a slacker friend. I better turn those notifications on.

Zane: Just completed the survey!

Tobias: Yes! Doing it now.

Simon: Should we all do it?

Hero: NO!

Beck: Can I use this in a book?

Graham: No, dibs!

. . .

I've just muted the group text when a call comes through. Jeez, what does Zane want now? To tease me some more?

"What?" I answer as the announcement calls for preboarding.

"Please tell me this was Nora's idea."

"Of course it was her idea. I would never do this to myself."

"And you went with it?"

"Nora …" I trail off. I'm about to defend her choices. "Knows what she's doing, all right. If she thinks this will work for me, so do I."

A long pause fills the line.

"Do you like her again?" he asks much more seriously.

Zane is the only one who even knew I had a crush on her back in college. You know, after I stood her up and pretended like I didn't like her. Zane knew.

"No," I answer quickly. Maybe too quickly.

"Right. I don't believe you. Do you think this will cause any problems?"

"No." Again, I answer quickly.

"Hero, be straight with me. This is Nora we are talking about."

"Exactly. She and I have a professional relationship only. Look, I have to go. See you on the tour?'

He sighs. "Yep. See you there."

We hang up, and my group number is called.

I only look back twice for Nora.

Where is she?

CHAPTER TEN

NORA

I barely make it to the gate on time. Truthfully, I sort of wish I hadn't. Yeah, professional Nora would have been disappointed, but personal Nora would have been pleased at Hero Quinn not getting his way. I bet he's panicking that I'm not here yet. Doug told me he's very specific about flying. Shows up two hours before his flight, except in Wind Valley because it's so small, always has a carry-on, always asks for the aisle seat because the window makes him sick, and so on.

Yeah, Hero Quinn is probably freaking out at this moment. And I need him to freak out. Once we were on a roll designing this survey at the coffee shop, I felt it again, that pull Hero has on me. It's so easy to be around him. So yeah, I need him to be upset with me. As long as we don't get along, things will be great.

Damn. I have got to stop referring to him by his full name. It's getting out of hand. Hero. He's just Hero.

I hold the face of my phone down on the scanner and wait for the approving beep before I board the plane. As soon as I have the go-ahead, I walk swiftly down the jet bridge. No doubt I'm the only person not on the plane at this point.

My assumptions are confirmed when rows of passengers are looking at me. Well, everyone except one. Which is probably why he stands out. Hero is in the third row. It's first class, and his seat is the only one in his row with the window shade pulled down.

His glances up and forces a smile.

I look to the seats across from him and then down to my ticket. I'm in row twenty-three. What the hell?

"Better find your seat."

"Clearly." I take a step and then stop. "I thought we could get some work done while the plane was in the air, but I see that won't work."

"I don't feel like trading with anyone in economy, and I guarantee no one up here is going to trade you. Maybe if you showed up early enough, we could've upgraded you."

I've had clients who have tested me, but Hero hits a whole new level. It's not even the fact we aren't sitting together. I don't need first class. But I didn't plan on following any of my clients for two entire weeks. And Hero is a last-minute addition, so developing this social media package with him is the task I have to squeeze into spare moments.

Like flight time.

Looks like I'll be focusing on a different client for this first flight. When we land though, I'll make sure Doug knows that our seats need to be next to each other from here on out. I don't like to waste time that can be used wisely.

I find my seat, sandwiching myself by the window. Row twenty-three is definitely in the back, but there are at least seven more to hit the bathrooms. I'd say that's luck.

The takeoff is smooth, and before I know it, we are given the go-ahead to work on laptops. I plop the table down in front of me and open my computer. The first thing that pops up is the cover of a steamy romance novel.

“Oh dear lord, please tell me you aren’t planning to watch a porno on this flight,” the elderly woman next to me says loudly. So loudly that she’s gaining the attention of more than one row around us.

“No, ma’am, I'm not. I’m just working.”

“On making a porno?”

The pure horror on her face would be comical if she weren't drawing more and more attention.

“On marketing a romance novel,” I say and turn my computer as best I can to shield her eyes from the screen.

She lets out a huff and twists to face the aisle. “I’d like to switch seats,” she says to the flight attendant. “My seatmate is watching an obscene movie.”

“I’m not watching an obscene movie. I’m working on marketing a book from a client who writes steamy romance. There is a big difference.”

The flight attendant gives me a soft smile. “I’ll see if there are any seats available in the front.”

In all actuality, I won't be sad if my so-called seatmate gets to move.

Sadly, two hours later and the old bat next to me is still in her place, and I'm ready to get off this plane.

“How was the flight?” Hero asks, surprisingly waiting for me to step off the jet bridge.

I force a smile. “It was marvelous.”

He chuckles and scratches his neck.

“Let’s get your bags.”

He turns and walks away, but I stay put.

I honestly can’t figure this one out. He was snappy and cocky before the flight took off and now he’s all … what? I don't even know. Normal.

This is going to be a long couple of weeks.

I pick up my pace to catch up with him and we walk in silence to baggage claim.

"So, do you fly to all your destinations, or do you drive to any? I noticed there are a few free times on this tour between signings. Do you actually take days off like you mentioned at the coffee shop, or do you fly home?"

Hero moves out of a rushing passenger's way. "I like to incorporate some type of vacation into these weeks. So on the days I'm not required to be anywhere, I do something fun."

"Oh."

"I know I requested for you to be here the entire time, but on the days where you can fly home, you should. If we aren't working, I don't want you to think you have to stick around."

I shrug. "I might do that, but a couple of the cities could be fun." Like Dallas and Seattle. A little sightseeing is definitely in my plans if I can help it.

My bag appears, so I move around Hero to grab it. Only, another man steps in front of me, so I have to reroute to get my bag. Then another person cuts me off. I start dodging people, trying to reach my bag but failing miserably. Why can't people just wait in one spot for their bag? This is ridiculous. When I finally catch up to it, it's heavier than I remember, so it jerks me forward. I'm fully prepared to fall on my face, but suddenly a hand covers mine and tugs on my bag.

The wheels hit the floor, and I don't even have to turn around to know who the body flush against my backside belongs too.

He smells just like he did back in college. Clean and minty.

I take a deep breath, and I swear my lips smile on their own.

Oh, this is not good.

I need to find him a girlfriend ASAP. Fooling around with a client—whom I don't want to even like—wouldn't look good on either of us.

Hero doesn't move immediately, and my confused heart reads too much into it.

Does he want to be this close? If so, why did he stand me up on our date?

As soon as he moves, I know those are all questions I'll never have an answer to. Which, to be honest, is for the best.

CHAPTER ELEVEN

HERO

Well, that was smooth. I basically rubbed my body against Nora's at the O'Hare baggage claim and didn't even apologize. She also didn't call me out on it, so maybe I'm the only one who was overthinking it.

Overthinking in more ways than one. God, her skin is soft. And my body reacted on cue. It wasn't even in a sexual way, yet my mind raced with all the ways to change that.

Jesus, I need to pull myself together.

I splash water on my face and look into the mirror.

Even though we just got here, my first blind date is tonight.

Nora was raving about it the entire Uber ride to the hotel, but Doug was here and so were some other clients of hers, so her attention drifted elsewhere, which is fine.

I didn't request her to be here to follow me around. Well, sort of. I'm fully aware that I'm not her only priority.

Anyway, she emailed me about an hour ago and said that we needed to meet in the lobby at 5:00 p.m.

It's 4:45, and my stomach is growling. I'm ready to go on

this date and get some food. Today has been a fast day of flying, a book signing, and now, finally, the first date.

I pop out of my room, pulling the door shut just as the door next to me opens.

Nora.

I'm not surprised we are near each other. I'm sure Doug books all of us on the same floor.

"Hi," she says, looking me over. "You look nice."

"Thank you." I take in her mid-thigh, blue spring dress and white sneakers. How she makes them look perfect with a dress is impressive. They must be her favorite pair of shoes. "You look nice as well. Plans tonight?"

"Just dinner," she says as we wait for the elevator. "Are you ready for this?"

I nod. "As ready as I can be."

"Perfect."

We share simple conversation, nothing too engrossing as we reach the lobby and take our Uber the short ten-minute drive to our location.

"Where am I meeting her?" I ask as we get out. We are close to Navy Pier with the Ferris Wheel behind us and many, many restaurants round us. Damn, those burgers at that grill across the street smell amazing. This might not be so bad after all.

"She's over there." Nora points to an outdoor space filled with workout equipment. Just beyond it is the water.

"A waterfront date?" I ask. "Is the food already there?"

"You'll get to eat, don't worry."

I nod but hesitate.

"Do I just walk over there?"

"Yep. I'll snap some pictures of you heading that way and when she meets you. I think keeping this distance angle is best. It's like a glimpse into the date without being right in your face."

"That's a good idea."

"Thanks."

Our eyes meet, but she looks away quickly and nods toward where I should head. "You better go. Don't want to be late."

"Right," I say but still hesitate. I lock my gaze on Nora's bright blue eyes. She licks her lip, pulling on the bottom one with her teeth, and I have the urge to forget about all this.

But it's her company's reputation and my career's. I can't back out.

I move slowly, waving goodbye to her. I swear the look on her face says she doesn't want me to go either.

I turn quickly.

There isn't anything you can do about her, Hero.

Still, I look back one last time. Nora hits me with a giant smile. She wiggles her fingers in goodbye just as someone hands her a to-go box.

Damn. Now I really want to be with her more. I'm hungry.

"Hero?" a woman calls out behind me.

I twist around and nod. "That's me. You must be Melanie."

She's got long, brown hair pulled back into a tight ponytail and is dressed in activewear. She's wearing a headset, which is sort of odd, but I'm not one to judge.

"Yep, and you're late," she says, reaching for me. "Those jeans will be brutal, and those will fully suck to wear." She points to my shoes. "I guess tennis shoes are better than nothing. Next time, there are shoes made for this, just FYI. There is your bike," she says and walks right by me.

My throat goes dry.

Oh no. No, no, no.

I'd noticed the spin bikes before, but I assumed we'd walk by them. To. Get. Food.

"Is everyone ready? We need to get this over with so I can go on my date with Hero Quinn!"

A collective cheer rings out.

“On your bike, Quinn,” Melanie repeats.

I’m too stunned to say anything, so I just do what I'm told. Melanie starts screaming orders.

This time, Nora is laughing as she snaps a couple pictures and takes a giant bite of her burger.

Oh hell.

She wasn’t sad to see me go. She’s out for revenge.

CHAPTER TWELVE

NORA

My heart won't stop racing.

The complete horror that took over Hero's face when he realized he was going to be working out during his date after he'd been counting down the minutes to food. The way that line between his eyes crinkled so badly I could see it through my lens from across the street. And when I took a bite of my burger under his watch.

It was perfect.

Day. Made.

I hadn't planned for the date to be a workout, I swear. The gal reached out to say a coworker had a last-minute cancelation and was curious if Hero would mind changing up their plans. Yes, I should have told him, so he could've worn something more appropriate, but a part of me—a petty part—wanted him to see what it felt like to go on a date and not get what you were expecting.

I let out an evil little laugh as I edit the video of him. It wasn't much. Mainly just him walking up to his date and their meet and greet. A little proof for his social account, and I was sure to cut it off as soon as he spun around to scold me. I'll be getting photos for the rest of his dates, but a video felt more fitting for this one since it wasn't a sit-down dinner.

I add a few fun captions before I submit the post and share it to his stories with a big sticker on it. I can't wait to see the insights for the next two weeks. I will admit that I spent more time than I normally do reviewing his status. His profile views blast some of my other clients out of the water. I was a bit surprised when I saw that his views overall had increased since his last release. I can't tell if that's because of the review and people want to check him out or something else. Natalie let it slip that his sales have dropped since the review. So my guess is, people are looking him up to be nosey.

I tap my chin as I think. There has to be something I'm missing. Or is it really as simple as a reader reading the L-Mag's review, stalking him on social media, and then deciding that the reviewer knows all, and Hero isn't worth the chance?

Gosh, that's so sad if that's the case.

Despite tonight's date—which to be fair, Hero works out a lot; anyone with eyes can see that—he could be having the time of his life, and I think it's very likely for Hero to—

"Nora!" Hero shouts from the other side of my door before he knocks. Loudly. "Open this door."

I cringe and practically hold my breath. He doesn't know I'm in here. I could be out at a bar or doing anything else but hiding in my room.

Also, it never crossed my mind that he would just show up after his date. We didn't plan that. He can share with me whatever details he needs to over breakfast tomorrow. Then again, I have a pretty good suspicion that he isn't here to share the highlights of his evening. It seems I didn't fully think about the consequences of my actions.

Okay, think. Don't move, don't breathe, and he will go away.

"Nora! I'll just wait right here till you open this door. I don't even care if you are not there. I'm not moving from this spot until we talk. If anyone can hear me. I'm not leaving until Nora speaks to me!"

Damn it.

Why is he so stubborn?

Oh, I don't know, Nora. Maybe because you told him he was going on a dinner date and then sent him to a cycle class with reviews that repeatedly said it was hell.

I let out a strangled sigh and get up for the door. At this rate, he's going to disturb the entire floor.

"Hey, Hero. How's it going?"

Oh god. *Do not laugh. Do not laugh. Do not do it.* He's bright red and drenched with sweat. His hair looks like he just got out of a swim, and his dress shirt is clinging to his body, outlining every hard pec and solid ripple across his chest. Wow. It's like some type of hidden superhero is standing in front of me. I want to reach out and touch him.

"You did that on purpose," he growls, pushing past me and marching into my room.

"What happened to you?" I ask, not smiling. Despite how badly I want to.

He spins on his heel, hands on his hips. "You. You happened to me."

I pinch my lips together to keep from smiling.

"I'm not sure I follow."

Yeah, playing dumb works.

"You came up with this whole entire idea, and I just spent the last hour and a half doing a cycle class in eighty-degree weather!"

Yikes. Ninety minutes of cycling. If anything, at least this date has successfully kept up my ruse of hating him, and clearly, he's not being pleased with me.

I busy myself with opening one of the water bottles in the mini fridge and taking a sip.

"Not only did I have to participate in her classes, but she used me as an example of what not to wear for a workout. She pointed out the outline of my butt sweat, Nora. My. Butt. Sweat."

The water in my mouth sprays all over him.

His eyes go wide as he looks at me, but I have no doubt that mine are wider. I totally just spit all over him.

"Refreshed?" I ask.

He closes his eyes to take a breath, and I have to force myself not to let my eyes wander.

"What the hell, Nora?"

All right, all right. I never said I was perfect.

"Your followers are going to eat this up," I tell him and then return to my seat at the table with my computer. "We should do an after-date interview."

I quickly pull up a Word doc and start listing out some questions I'd come up with earlier. I'd planned to mention this to him in the morning at either breakfast or on our flight. Chicago is our shortest stop on this tour. I'm not opposed to it. The last three are longer and hold more interest for me anyway.

"Should we just do a typical Q and A, or should we do a scale type thing? Live would be awesome, or should we—"

"I don't feel like you're listening to me," Hero cuts me off and sits on the edge of my bed. "I don't want to talk about my date. I want to talk about how you deliberately set me up to fail today."

"I did no such thing."

But maybe I did. I just thought it would be fun. I didn't think anyone would look at this as a failure. But he clearly does, and he's not totally wrong. The next one will be better. It has to be. For both of us.

"And don't even get me started on anyone eating anything

up. I still haven't had dinner." He tugs at his hair and groans. "Look, we can dance around this for however long you'd like, but even if you don't like me, this is my career, Nora. It's yours too. We need to make this work."

"It is working."

"Is it, though?"

"Yes." I click to a different tab on my browser and turn my computer. The post I made only minutes ago about this date already has more likes than his last week of posting combined.

He moves to stand next to me.

"Look at that. Your readers love seeing you make an effort."

Hero crosses his arms and widens his stance.

"That doesn't prove anything."

"No? Then read the comments." I point to my computer, but it's clear he doesn't plan on getting any closer.

I roll my eyes. "Fine. I'll read you a few."

I scan the list that continues to grow. "Oh, this one: I once went out with a guy who owned a gym. He made me sign up for a membership before we went on our first date. My advice on this one is simple: run as fast as you can."

I look at him with a smile. He's still glaring.

"Okay, what about this one: I totally had a workout as a first date once, and I'll tell you, I'm pretty sure the way I run is exactly why he didn't call me back. He commented on it at least three times during the date. Good luck to you. I've been there." I clap as soon as I'm done reading that one. "Your date tonight made you relatable, Hero. Readers love knowing they have something in common with you. And guess what—you aren't the only person out there to have a bad date."

The expression on his face softens, but I can tell by the look in his eyes that he isn't fully convinced. "You can't be perfect right out of the gate, Hero. If all this goes too easy for you, they will think it's staged. This is real." I repeat the word for emphasis. "Readers want real."

This time, he lets out a sigh and sits back on my bed.

"Fine. What you're saying makes sense, but does the next one have to be so … exhausting?"

"I'll see what I can do."

He nods, looking around my room. I fail to not let my eyes wander this time. If I took a post-date picture of him like this, yeesh, I bet it would go viral. As much as I hate to admit it, guys with bodies like Hero's … well, they bring attention, and it's great at—

"Nora?" Hero says, snapping his finger in front of me. "Did you hear me?"

Definitely did not, no.

"How are you reviewing them anyway?" he asks, shifting again from the bed to the chair next to me. He leans in to look at my computer. "Let's look at one now."

I close my laptop.

"I think the element of surprise is key here."

He groans.

"So you're not going to show me any of the applicants?"

"Nope."

I don't want him picking a date. What if he deliberately chooses the wrong gal? As long as I'm choosing, I stand a chance that he'll meet someone.

"Please."

I shake my head. "No begging is going to get me to change my mind."

"What if I grovel?" he asks, winking and looking right into my eyes.

I don't have an answer. I'm too stunned by how close he is. I knew he was sitting next to me, but I didn't process how close till just now. Till he winked and his leg touched mine. Till he bumped me with his shoulder, and I felt his deep chuckle all the way to my core.

"The answer will still be no."

Yeah, girl, hold it together!

"Damn. Is this why they call you the best?'

"Pretty much, yes." I stand. "We should probably get to bed. The flight tomorrow is early, and we should both be well rested."

I move to the door and open it for him.

"How about you just ride with me? I have a car already scheduled to pick me up in the morning at seven."

"That sounds great."

"Cool. See you in the morning."

"Good night."

He hesitates in the doorway.

"Something else?" I ask.

He smiles but shakes his head. "Nope."

And we stand here like two fools who can't stop smiling at each other.

So, obviously, I do what any sane girl would do at this moment.

I close the door in his face.

CHAPTER THIRTEEN

HERO

I didn't sleep well last night. It wasn't because I'm not in my own bed or that my body hurt from my date, because it did, and it's not because being on tour stresses me out. Nope. It was because of Nora.

I was too busy trying to tell myself that crushing on her again isn't a wise idea. First of all, I'm her client, which I clearly need to keep repeating to myself. Second of all, she is my agent's cousin. Third, and most important, she hates me.

However, last night, I feel like something may have shifted between us. I can't quite put my finger on it, but something changed.

And that feeling—god, that feeling, it was like being back in college and seeing her for the first time. My heart raced, my palms grew sweaty, and my brain quit processing words.

My body didn't want to talk at all. I'm drawn to this woman in every way possible. And it wasn't like I was going to tell her this. I was too busy scolding her for the date she set me up on.

I check my emails as I wait in the lobby for the car that's taking us to the airport. We have a flight today and a small signing this afternoon in Dallas. Tomorrow is a larger meet and greet followed by date number two. Clearly, I need to be ready for anything.

We are about to be together on a plane for quite a few hours, so that should be plenty of time to sway this next date in my favor. Especially since I had Doug upgrade her ticket to sit with me this time.

"Your car to the airport should be ready for you at the front desk," Doug says into the phone. He'd had me on hold while he checked to see where the car was. It's almost 7:20, and they are late. "I'm not sure what the hold-up is, but it's there."

"Great, thanks for checking on that for me. I know it's not part of your job description."

"You're my best client, Hero. I'm happy to help."

"I'm sure you say that to all your clients."

"Guilty. Okay, look. Zane is meeting you this afternoon. Your signings are back-to-back. I also messaged Nora that the car is ready now. She appreciated the heads up and extra few minutes to get ready."

"Awesome. Thank you. What time does Zane get in?" I like nothing more than having one of my best friends around when I'm on tour.

"One, I think. You'll have to ask him. You should all get there about the same time."

This is perfect. Just enough time to grab lunch. I have a new plot idea I'd like to run by him. The group has been toying with the idea of writing a series together. A six-book series in which we each write one book. I have an idea for it.

"Thanks again, Doug. I'll let you know when we get there."

"Perfect. Oh, and great news: I checked stats this morning and the numbers went up on your sales and sales rank overnight. Not by a landslide, but enough to put your name back on some charts. Whatever Nora did for you with this first date, keep it up. It's doing something."

"That's great, Doug."

"Travel safe and don't let Nora boss you around too much."

He clicks off just as the elevator doors glide open to reveal Nora and her gold rolling suitcase.

She gives me a small wave and heads in my direction.

"Were you waiting long?"

"Nope. Care to tell me about my next date?"

"Nope," she says, tugging her bag behind her toward checkout.

That's fine. She doesn't have to tell me. I have a whole list of questions for her in my notebook. Since I couldn't sleep, I made good use of my time.

"Your car is here, Mr. Quinn," the receptionist says as he approaches me.

"Thank you," I say, pulling my bag behind me. Nora is right on my heel.

"Let me guess, while you were on the phone with Doug, you had him change my seat on the flight again to punish me for your date last night."

I bit my lip to hide my smile. Technically, I didn't request that he move her seat the first time. I'm not sure what happened there. All I know is, I fully expected her to sit with me on the flight, and Doug was the one who informed me that her seat was changed.

"Actually, I had him upgrade you to sit with me."

"Damn it," she says, her arms dropping to her sides in defeat as the driver lifts her bag into the back of the car. "You do want to punish me."

I pause halfway into the car. She's full of some spunk today, isn't she? Again, I hold back my smile. "I'm sorry. Sitting with me is punishment?"

"The worst kind. It's going to be three hours of you begging to see your date lineup." She, too, hops into the back seat as I buckle my seat belt.

"I actually had another plan for the flight."

She side-eyes me, picking at something on her leggings. "Like what?"

"I made a list of questions I'd like you to give me answers to."

She groans, dropping her face into her hands. "Can you drive by a Starbucks or someplace with coffee?" she asks the driver. "I'm clearly going to need it."

"Sure thing, ma'am."

"No, no stops. We are already cutting it close."

"We have two hours before our flight even boards, Hero."

"About an hour and half now that the car was late."

I can feel her watching me as I check my phone to be sure nothing with our flight has changed.

"Coffee, please," Nora says, ignoring me.

"No coffee."

"You know, ma'am," the driver speaks up. "My sister owns her own little coffee hut that is on the way and would take less time than finding a chain cafe."

Nora looks at me with a wide grin. Despite the scowl I'm giving her, her smile doesn't budge.

"We would love to support your sister, wouldn't we, Hero?"

Oh, her spunk is thick. As someone who has built a career off being self-made, she knows there is no way I can say no.

I nod. "Yes, we would."

"Perfect!" she says and pulls out her phone. "Now I just need to pull up the airline app."

"Why? I checked us in this morning."

As soon as the words are out of my mouth, I adjust myself in the seat and focus straight ahead. I said that way too fast. My brain sort of short-circuited there.

"To see about changing my seat," she informs me.

"Oh."

Well, damn. She really doesn't want to sit by me. Another great reminder of why this crush I have for her needs to be cut off right now. Since Nora has been back in my life, I let myself believe that maybe, just maybe, there could be something between us. Like last night when I was leaving her room. God, I swear there was a moment. Clearly, I was wrong.

"Hey," she says softly, her hand resting on my thigh. "I'm kidding."

My eyes find hers, and just like last night, my heart races. I can't be the only one who feels it. Her gaze quickly drops to her hand, and she jerks it back. "I'm so sorry. That was inappropriate."

I clear my throat. Nothing about that was inappropriate. What was, though, are my thoughts of other things she could be doing with that hand or that we could be doing in the back seat. Her in my lap, facing me, and my hand exploring her body as I listen to the noises she makes when I touch her.

"It wasn't," I tell her.

"It was. Why don't we get started on your list of questions?"

I shake my head. "Let's wait for the plane."

"And coffee. Good plan," she agrees.

By the time we are through security and our group is being called to board, my mind is still confused. Am I thinking of Nora in this light because she's put me in a situation to be thinking about attraction? Perhaps I'm just lusting for her. She is the one who got away, which makes my reaction natural.

Still. No matter how many times I try to talk myself out of it, my instincts keep telling me to do more. I can't not do something. What if I'm never in a position like this with her again? What if this is my one chance to get to know her?

I glance at my watch as we board the plane.

Lunch. Lunch with Zane is good. I need advice.

What am I going to do about Nora?

CHAPTER FOURTEEN

NORA

I have no idea how I'm going to fly anything but first class ever again.

"Would you like another glass of wine, miss?"

"Yes, please," I reply without missing a beat as I hand her my empty glass, reaching across Hero's face.

He lets out a small chuckle. "Nora, you do realize it's only nine in the morning, right?"

"Mm-hmm," I say, pulling my iPad from my large purse.

"And you're on glass number two."

"And?"

I glance at him, keeping the expression on my face mute. I have nothing scheduled today beyond saying hello to a client here or there at a signing. Why not drink at nine in the morning? It makes perfect sense for a travel day if you ask me. Plus, our next hotel has a pool, and we will be there for three days. I plan to have this second glass now and then be poolside with a whole new round of beverages, all while Hero prepares for his next signing.

"Nothing." He shakes his head. "Your confidence in drinking this early is intriguing."

"Well, your next signing isn't until tomorrow afternoon. If you want a drink, I'm sure you'd be just fine. Do you want to try my wine?"

"Nope," he says, pulling out a notebook. Like a legit pen and paper notebook. I glance from my piece of technology to his college ruled paper. Do all writers just always have a notebook on hand?

"Are you ready for my questions?" he asks just as my drink arrives. Talk about perfect timing. I have a feeling I'm going to need a little more liquid courage for this.

"Hit me."

"Why don't you like me?"

I choke on the liquid that fails to go down, causing Hero to reach around me to pat my back. He was certainly ready.

"I'm good," I say through a cough. "I'm good."

"Perfect. I'll wait for the answer while you catch your breath."

"I feel like choking earned me a pass."

"Nope. I need to know the answers so we can move on."

Does he really need me to answer that? He's a smart man. He knows what he did. I narrow my gaze at him as I lower my glass to the small table in front of me.

"If I have to tell you, we have bigger problems to fix."

He lets out an exaggerated sigh.

"Nora, I am truly sorry I stood you up that night."

The edge in his voice is sincere.

"Thank you."

"You're welcome."

"Why did you do it?" The words are out of my mouth before I can stop them. It's too late. They're out there now. No turning back.

"I, um..." He rubs his neck and starts flipping through his notebook as if the answer were written inside. "That's a tough one to answer."

"Really?" I huff-laugh. "Because from my view, you stood me up so you could make out with some sorority girl. That's where I found you after I left the restaurant."

He cringes. "Trust me, that was not why I wasn't there."

"Then enlighten me."

"I just ... it's complicated."

"Oh, solid choice of words from a professional writer. I think you're stalling to think of an excuse."

"I was there. I was at the restaurant. I just never made it to the table." He pauses, but honestly, what would I say to that? This is definitely something I didn't know.

He closes his eyes and shakes his head.

"You know what? Let's just get to work. You like to work on flights, right?"

His tone is a clear invitation to change the subject, and since he is, in fact, right about my joy in working during flights and it's clear there is something I'm unaware of about that night, I pull out my computer instead.

He was there at the restaurant? Did he feel the same connection I did and freak out? Was there an emergency in his family? I should have talked to him back then, but I was too stubborn.

I want to ask him about it so badly.

But if he wants to work, let's work.

"So after the post blew up last night, and considering we are in Dallas for a few days, I think we should wait to post until after you leave each event. So, be sure to check in with me when you get back to the hotel every night, and then I'll post everything from that day. The signing, tour stuff, and the date. How does that sound?"

"My readers will be more engaged in real time."

"Well, we didn't exactly do real time on the first date."

"Exactly. We never discussed it."

Whoa. Hello, snappy Hero.

"We could have if we had time to work on things during the flight," I point out.

"Not this again."

I take a breath and look out the window. I swear, he says things like that just so he can get a rise out of me. The fact that he somehow knows me well enough to do that is equally annoying.

"All right." He claps his hands. "I'm really ready now." He flags down the flight attendant. "Can I get a drink?"

"Wow, Hero, you do realize it's not even noon yet, right?" My voice is full of teasing, but he misses it completely. Talk about a failure to lighten the mood.

After his drink arrives, we dive into a social media routine for the next quarter. We discuss features for his books and a few other advertising opportunities we both agree need to be run by Doug before we commit.

All in all, it's a successful flight, and before I know it, we are working independently. His fingers are sweeping over the keyboard of his small laptop as he writes a new book. I keep stealing glances, but each time I do, he pauses and looks at me.

Eventually, I control myself. It helps that Hero closes his computer and puts on some headphones to watch a movie.

I slide on my own headphones. Hero has given me a lot to work with. Between the things we just went over and the dates, this new, softer side of him that his readers will see will boost his image online and spur sales more than we originally thought.

Before I know it, the flight attendant is announcing our descent. I lean toward Hero to see if there is anything else he wants to go over before we land. His head bobs for a moment before flopping to rest on my shoulder. I notice immediately that his eyes are closed.

I sit ramrod straight.

Hero Quinn is asleep on my shoulder, and holy moly, is he gorgeous when he sleeps. He looks so gentle and he's so quiet.

I like this version of him.

I would have liked the younger version of him had I given him another chance. It's amazing how one can choose to react when they are hurting, and it's clear from our unsuccessful conversation earlier that I don't have all the pieces to the story. Even though I still feel that he owes me an explanation, it's exhausting pretending to dislike someone this long.

I look down at his sleeping face.

From this moment forward, Hero will get normal Nora. You know what else he's going to get? A girlfriend. I started this event for him, and I'm going to see it through. That's what a friend would do.

CHAPTER FIFTEEN

HERO

I love book signings, but there is peace in knowing that I'm headed to lunch with Zane. It's something we do back home at least twice a week, so it feels familiar.

I need familiar right now.

My mind is all over the place. It helps that Nora and I did tighten up some plans with this survey. From now on, we will go to the dates together. She will capture a picture of me and my date (with the date's approval, of course), and then she will hang in the background sneaking photos for a bit before leaving. After, if it's not too late, we will meet up to discuss and plan a postdate post for my online accounts.

Maybe we needed to get the first one out of the way to see what my readers wanted, because the new details make me eager to give this another go. I should consider having Nora add one more date to the list, since the first one was a flop.

Yet even though the career side of my life feels balanced, the rest of it does not. I feel like I'm being pulled in twenty different directions, and I never know what to expect when I'm with Nora. Especially after the flight earlier. Things were good and then they weren't. That's my fault, to be fair. I just feel so out of control with her. *She* makes me feel out of control, and it's only been two days.

Hell, maybe out of control isn't even the right phrase to use. She … she ... this! This is what she does to me. I can't think straight.

I walk into the bar and grill that's connected to our hotel, spotting Zane right away. He's in his signature outfit. A simple T-shirt that might be a little snug on his biceps, a pair of jeans, and sneakers. Oddly enough, they're exactly what I'm wearing.

Are we those friends, seriously? We hang out so often that we've start to morph into one and are now showing up to places with the same exact shoes on.

"Nice kicks," I say and drop into the chair across from him.

He leans over the edge of the table to look and then erupts into laughter that draws attention.

"Why do we always do this?" he asks.

"I have no clue."

"At least we have good taste," he says just as the waitress appears. We order our drinks and talk about our morning and browse the menu. As soon as we've put in our orders and the nachos we ordered as an appetizer show up, I lean back in my chair.

"So, I want to ask you something."

"Okay." He takes a bite of the chip in his hand but watches me warily.

"It's about Nora."

Zane takes another bite but doesn't speak.

"Are you listening?" I lean forward and keep my voice down.

He nods. "Yes. I'm just waiting for you to go on."

"Oh." I scratch the back of my neck. "Well, do you remember my first book?"

He nods as he finishes chewing. "You mean, do I remember the book that you wrote after you fell for Nora and never told her? Yeah, I do."

"Say it a little louder, why don't you?"

"Why are you asking?"

I shift in my seat.

"Well, you know Doug hired her to help with my reputation and she's tagging along through my tour."

Zane nods.

I take a deep breath and close my eyes. *Just say it.* "Those feelings are back."

My best friend chokes on his next bite.

That's two for two today. I'm on a roll with my topics, it seems.

"Shit. I knew it. Are you serious?"

"Yes. And I want to tell her, but it seems complicated with this whole dating survey thing."

He looks over each of his shoulders and then whispers, "Is she here now?"

I nod. "In her room, I bet. Maybe by the pool. I don't know. She doesn't exactly run her play- by-play by me."

"Shit."

"Yeah."

"So things are going well then?"

"Well." I blow out a breath. "I'm struggling with how to determine if her feelings match mine. She's a tough nut to crack. One minute I think she's into me, and the next I have no clue."

Zane snorts with a laugh.

"What?"

"You stood her up on a date, Hero. People, man or woman, don't forget that kind of humiliation."

"It's been years."

Then again, she did ask me why on the plane, so maybe she

isn't over it. How can I develop an entire heroine in a book and not be able to figure this out?

"All right," Zane says, leaning back as the waitress switches our nachos out for our food. "Let's say she's over it. Obviously, based on how you two acted at Tobias's birthday, she doesn't care for you that much. What would be the reason?"

I shrug. "I don't know."

He doesn't give me time to think more on it.

"I have a theory. In college, we were those guys who wrote romance, Hero. The women loved us in college, and we loved them."

He's not wrong. I did go off on a binge of sorts when Nora wouldn't give me the time of day. I had to get her out of my head.

Zane starts to chuckle loudly.

"What now?"

"I was just thinking about the night after your botched date. The night you tried to apologize to Nora, and she shut you down. It was the first night you told anyone not in our group that you wrote romance. Man, the girls flocked to you, and you hadn't even been published yet."

I shake my head and grin. I'm not proud of all the choices I made in college, but we did have some good times. And yet, Zane might be onto something. Has Nora not liked me for skipping out on our date or for the way I acted after? She mentioned both on the plane. Neither were my best moments.

"Either way, I'm in over my head, and I'm a little terrified for the date she's going to send me on tomorrow night." I give him a quick recap of my first date night's events.

When he finally stops laughing, he says, "Yeah, I'd be worried too."

"Oh, Hero, there you are." Nora steps into view. "I wanted to run an idea by you." She stops to stand at our table. Her hair is pulled back into a high, loose bun with stray pieces of hair surrounding her face, and she's changed into a pair of camo-green cotton shorts with a white blouse and black wedges. Her lips are a dark pink, and I can't seem to pull my eyes away from them as she speaks.

Zane kicks my foot under the table.

"Huh?"

Nora glares at me. "Zane, it's good to see you again."

"Nora." He nods. "Always a pleasure."

"Don't forget to send me your next month's promotions schedule. Yours is the only one I don't have," she says, directing her attention to Zane.

"You'll have it as soon as we're done with lunch."

"Thank you. Congratulations on your latest release. I heard you hit number one in the first twenty-four hours of release."

"I did. Thank you. It's nice to know my work is appreciated. Makes me feel like I'm doing something right."

"I bet. So, Hero, how does my room sound? Tomorrow night? You'll be there?"

Now I'm really lost.

"What?"

"Seriously? We talked about this on the flight, and I just finished looking over how this post- date interview will work, if we want to go that route. I still think you should consider it."

Oh, right, the post-date interview. I vetoed the idea, but Nora is still pulling for it.

"That works for me. How late is too late to show up?"

She cocks her hip to the side. "Plan on staying out late, do you?"

"No. I just don't want to wake you if you've fallen asleep."

"You won't. I don't sleep well when I'm out of town, so I get a lot of work done. I'll be up."

"Noted."

“See you at the signing then.”

“Bye. Have a good tour, Zane.”

“Thanks,” he barely says before she's gone. With a glance over his shoulder to be sure she’s out of earshot, he laughs.

I’m glad I could entertain him during this lunch hour.

“I take back what I said about the date.”

“What do you mean?” I ask.

“You have bigger things to be worried about than some silly dates.”

“Like what?”

“Like what you’re going to do about Nora. If anything, I'd be worried that you’ll fall in love with her all over again.”

“I wasn't in love with her.”

“Are you sure?”

I take a deep breath, then resume eating my lunch.

If it wasn’t love, it was something damn near close.

CHAPTER SIXTEEN

HERO

I've made Nora laugh three times today.

Each time that sweet sound comes from her, it swallows me. I enjoy it more than I should. For the short time that she was at my signing table earlier, she seemed to be a big hit. She'd stopped by to pass on a message from Doug, but then a reader asked her a question about working with me and then so did the next and so on. The patience Nora had with each reader—clearly, she's done this before. Her smile when she said that I'm the client who keeps her the busiest, but for good reason, is one I'll never forget. Almost as if she were smiling because deep down, she loves working with me.

Wishful thinking on my part.

Still, this was one of my favorite signings ever.

That said, I'm also hoping my humor for the day has won her over and that she spares me on tonight's date. I'm not saying the last was intentional, but I'd really like for this one to go better.

But first, I need to finish this meet and greet at the bookstore.

"Oh my gosh, I loved *Mad Love*," the girl in front of me says. "I swear you wrote that book straight to my soul."

"I'm glad you enjoyed it."

I sign the book she gives me and then smile for a picture.

She squeals and practically sprints away. I glance up to try to gather a head count on how many people are left in line, and I spot Nora walking toward me.

"Is everything all set for tonight?" I ask her between readers.

"They are."

"Oh gosh, are you the one setting him up on these dates?" the current reader asks Nora as she hands me a book to sign.

"I am."

"Genius idea," another reader in line notes. See, she's a hit. "I can't wait to see him fall in love. I'm sure the list is so long that it's hard to pick the right girl for him. Someone so perfect and beautiful."

"It's a lot easier than you think," Nora replies, and I snort.

Both women look at me.

"Do you want me to personalize this?" I ask.

"Oh yes, please, my name is Kimmy."

"There you go, Kimmy." I hand the book back to her.

"Thanks!"

I secretly hope one of the readers will ask her what tonight's date entails, but they don't. As soon as the signing is over, Nora and I freshen up and then call a car to take us to my date.

"All right, so as we discussed, I'll get a picture of the two of you at the start, and then I'll be around to get more pictures, but you won't see me. Okay?"

"If I'm in a restaurant, I'll probably see you."

"I can be pretty sneaky," Nora says with a wink. "Oh, we're here!"

Once we're out of the car, we go our separate ways. On the flight to Dallas, Nora and I had agreed that she wouldn't wait for my date with me. That might make them nervous, so she'll introduce herself after we've ordered drinks.

I glance in the direction Nora went, but true to her word, I can't find her.

Well, here goes date number two. Wish me luck.

* * *

With sweaty palms, I wait for my date to arrive. To be safe, I did wear a pair of jeans that are a lot looser than the pair I wore on my first date.

She's five minutes late, and I won't be horribly upset if she doesn't show up. As thrilled as I am that that first date boosted my numbers, I'm nervous this will be just as disastrous as the last one. Two failed back-to-back dates would not make me look good.

"Oh!" A loud squeal fills the restaurant.

I glance up to see a woman jumping up and down and clapping.

"It's Hero Quinn!" she yells.

I hold my composure, but a small part of me dies inside as I wave at her. I may look like an extrovert on social media, but I'm a full-blown introvert to my core.

It's safe to say that blind dates are not my thing, and that this must be my date.

I rise out of the booth just as the loud woman and younger version of her approach me.

"Hi, are you Lily?" I ask the woman, but she just shakes her head and smiles. Then she points to the younger woman who is definitely closer to my age.

Lily's eyes are pressed closed, and her nose is scrunched up. "I'm Lily," she says. "And this is my mom, my aunt, and my sister." More of them appear.

Fuck.

"Oh my gosh, we are all so excited to be here and have

dinner with you and see you in real life." The mom pauses for only a brief moment to touch my arms. Her smile turns dead serious. "Wow."

"So you're looking to settle down?"

"How many kids do you want?"

"Will you always live in Wyoming?"

I can barely keep up with who is speaking.

"I want three kids, and I love Wyoming," my date says completely out of the blue. Then she looks at her mom, who nods in approval.

"We've never actually been to Wyoming," her mother chimes in.

"I'll like it. I know I will," one of the other women says.

"I don't trust him," the aunt, I think, says. "He's too quiet."

"Probably doesn't have time to get a word in with you including yourself in the conversation," the mom says.

The entire restaurant is staring at this point, so I remember why I'm doing this—the author of the year honor—and do what I do best.

I flash them a smile and flag down the waiter.

"Can we get a bigger table and your house red, please?"

"Right away, sir."

Lily eyes me skeptically. "You're not freaked out that my entire family is here?"

A little, but she doesn't need to know that.

"Nope. The more the merrier," I tell them as we find our new table.

Conversation comes easy with this group, and before I know it, we have our drinks and Lily's aunt is telling me all about how she wants to write a book someday.

"Hi," Nora says quietly as she approaches the table.

"Nora, perfect timing. Should we get a picture?"

The squeals that erupt will be hard to get used to.

Nora snaps the picture, her gaze connecting with mine when she's done. She nods once and then she's gone.

"Oh my gosh, did I tell you about the dream I had after I read *Mad Love*?" the cousin asks.

"No, tell me about it."

The remainder of the evening goes the same. Lots of questions and stories from Lily's family, and by the time we leave the restaurant to get ice cream, I'm pretty sure I've taken more than a hundred photos—every squeal brought new attention to me—and I'd been tagged in more than thirty photos. I'm pretty sure I know more about their family than I do my own.

There won't be a second date for Lily and me, but compared to date one, tonight was a complete win.

I glance at my watch to see it's just past ten.

Nora is surely still awake, right? She said she would be.

I searched for her a few times during dinner but never saw her. I could probably wait until tomorrow to find out what kind of feedback her posts are getting me, but I'll be honest, today was a good day, and the only person I want to share it with is Nora.

CHAPTER SEVENTEEN

NORA

The nerves that had built up as I waited for Hero's date to end vanished the moment he knocked on my hotel room door.

I open the door slowly, leaving the sliding bolt locked.

Yep, it's Hero.

Just like the first night, he's standing with his hand on his hips as he looks at me.

"Can I come in?" he asks slowly.

I back up and unlock the door fully.

"Do you—?"

"I just need a moment of silence," he says, plopping himself onto my side of the bed and making himself right at home.

Great. Now my sheets are going to smell like him.

I hide my smile. Worst things have happened.

He drapes a hand over his eyes—I take that as my cue to just wait.

So I get on my phone, which is on the bed next to him, take a seat there, and look up the insights on tonight's date post. I would have waited to post it, as planned, but he was tagged so many times by readers that hiding his location seemed pointless.

Also, it wasn't part of the plan for Lily to bring her entire family, and I have no doubt that Hero is about to blame me for this. So I'm going to assume that the whole live interview after the date is off the table.

"Look at this," I say and lean toward Hero. "More than six thousand views since I posted it a couple hours ago. This is unreal."

He groans and sits up on the bed.

"From tonight's date?"

"Yes! People are loving this whole family angle."

"Yeah, speaking of that—it was a bit much. Don't get me wrong, I enjoyed tonight, but will the next one be a date or a group gathering?"

"I had no idea she was bringing her family, but it sort of worked out for us. Oh, who are some of these other women who tagged you? Readers, I assume."

"Yep, just some random readers who came to say hi."

"Awe, that's cute." I turn back to my computer just as an email comes in from Doug.

"Oh my god!"

"What?" Hero says and rushes to the chair next to mine.

"L-Mag reached out to Doug about your survey. They want to do an interview with you."

"What?" He spins my computer to face him. "I've been on a whole whopping two dates." He reads the email and then pulls out his phone. "So, the L-Mag knows what I'm doing and likes it?"

"I'd say so."

"Do you know what this means?" He stands quickly and starts to pace, a smile forming on his lips. "This is working. This might actually work. I might still win author of the year."

He does a little dance and then fist pumps the air.

Oh my. He's freaking adorable when he's excited.

I can't help but smile as his energy fills the rooms.

"That would be pretty sweet."

"Yeah, it would. Should we schedule more dates?" he asks. "Oh! Group ones for sure."

More group dates? No, I need him to find a match, especially right now. This side of him is so fun that I can already feel myself falling. That can't happen.

I need to steer this back to finding him a girlfriend.

"Not to ruin the mood, but the point is to find a girlfriend. We should really focus on one-on-one dates."

He pauses for a moment, the smile on his lips dropping. He points his phone at me.

"Good point."

"I know."

He flashes me a forced grin and then sits back down, but this time on my bed again.

"How cool would it be if you actually fell in love on this book tour?" I ask, keeping my focus on the screen and the task at hand. Not on the fact that Hero Quinn is on my bed. "And then it was made into a movie or something."

"Yeah, that would be pretty sweet."

I don't miss the lack of excitement in his tone as he leans on my pillows, his eyes focused on my TV.

"What are you watching?" he asks.

Ah. And a change of subject. Hint taken. If he doesn't want to discuss his dating life, that is fine by me.

"Oh, I wasn't really watching anything. It was more background noise. But I think the show is called *Schitt's Creek*."

"Sounds interesting." He turns up the volume while I go back to working on my computer. Since I'm up, I might as well log in and check a few things. I posted to three accounts back-to-back. I need to make notes on whether they were optimal times or if I need to change when I post throughout the day.

"Don't you want to go back to your room to get some sleep? You have an early signing tomorrow," I suggest. It's the last one in Dallas, then we head to Denver the day after. He has the whole afternoon off tomorrow. What will he do with his free time?

"Why? Are you trying to kick me out of your room? The tours can be lonely. It's kind of nice to have someone else here. Even if she doesn't care for me."

My back is to him, so he can't see me cringe. All right, Hero isn't as awful as I wanted him to be, and he and I clearly have a similar thought process when it comes to success, but still. I hardly know him anymore, and it's not a wise idea to start. The less time we are together is probably best. In fact, the less time he spends on my bed, the better for me.

"What about Zane?" I ask. "Isn't he staying here tonight?"

Beck is here, too, but if Hero is going out late with anyone, it would be Zane.

"He went to a club."

My point exactly. He should be with him and not me.

"You didn't want to go?"

"I had a date, remember?"

"You could have gone after," I point out, still not looking away from my computer.

"Yeah, I guess, but I told you I'd be here and I am. I like to keep my word."

I slowly look back. His eyes find mine.

"All right, I keep my word *now*. You can hold it against me, but I did learn from that experience."

"I didn't say anything about it."

"You gave me a look."

"And you know what my looks mean?"

"I think so."

"Sure," I roll my eyes.

"That one says, 'Oh he thinks he's so smooth.'"

I burst into laughter. He's pretty close.

"Why don't you call it a night and come watch your show?" he asks.

"Because you're in my bed and I have work to do."

He holds my gaze but shakes his head. "You'll always have work to do."

"And you'll always have your bed in your room with your own TV and the same show if you leave."

He scoots off the bed.

"Fine. You win. I can be stubborn, but if anything, I listen." He moves for the door, and my heart is both racing with disappointment that he's leaving and relief.

"Breakfast tomorrow?" he asks, opening the door.

I follow behind him so I can lock it.

"I'll see you there."

"Perfect." He spins, not realizing I'm behind him. His arm brushes against my breasts, and immediately my heart races, my nipples go hard, and my breath hitches.

All that from one accidental touch. What's going to happen when he touches me intentionally?

He swallows and then looks into my eyes.

I lick my lips.

I'm about to find out.

His hand touches my hip, gently pulling me closer to him.

I put a hand on his chest and silently cheer at the feel of his body against mine and the overwhelming need that consumes me.

His eyes close, and even though I know it's crazy, I push away from him. "Have a good night, Hero."

His head dips, ready for a kiss that can't happen. Slowly, he looks up.

"You too, Nora."

His smile grows as he taps the doorframe twice before leaving.

As soon as the door shuts, I race to my bed and grab my phone to text Natalie.

I need advice.

CHAPTER EIGHTEEN

HERO

One of my favorite things about sharing my agent with friends is that Doug likes to schedule crossovers in our tours. An afternoon off with me and the boys all sitting poolside at the same hotel.

"We really should learn to take more vacations," Graham says.

"It's hard to take a vacation when we are all workaholics," Zane says.

To this, we all raise a bottle and drink.

"So," Tobias says, and I can tell from his tone that he's about to ask someone something they won't want to answer. Probably me.

"I'd like to know what's going on between Quinn and Grayson."

I knew it.

"Nothing is going on between me and Nora."

"That lie is just as big as that breath you just let out." Tobias pins me with a look. "Spill it."

"Yeah, spill," Zane teases. "He needs to go back to Natalie and gossip."

"I do not gossip with Natalie."

"All guys gossip with their girlfriends," Beck chimes in.

"It's like a written rule." This from Simon.

A flustered Tobias says, "Jesus Christ, you guys, Natalie isn't my girlfriend. We are just friends. I've been telling you this for years and years."

A string of "yeah rights" fall around us.

I chuckle, thankful for the change of subject.

Dodged a bullet right there.

"Shit, shit. Don't look, Hero. Don't look across the pool right now."

But, of course, I look. I spot Nora walking in a red swimsuit and white cover-up with big black sunglasses. Well, I think it's a cover-up—it looks more like one of my button-down shirts. She'd look good in one of those. Of mine, I mean. The one she has on is great too.

"Are you drooling?" Tobias asks.

"I'll get us more water." Zane chuckles, waving at one of the pool waiters.

"You guys suck," I say as Graham and Simon laugh.

"Hey, didn't you like love her back in college?" Simon asks.

I look straight ahead, expressionless. Why is this happening to me?

"No."

"You went on that one date with her, right?" Beck asks. "Was it like kismet and only you felt it?"

"He never made it," Tobias says with some snark. "Natalie didn't talk to me for a whole week because of that."

A memory he will never let me forget.

"It didn't work out." I shift to grab my iPad and pull up a Google document. This entire tour has given me some pretty good ideas for my next series. Nora will know where I got the inspiration, but I'm sure she'll pretend like she doesn't.

"You like her." Graham sits up, his voice serious. "Don't you?"

The next to sit up is Simon, followed by Beck and Zane. Tobias is on the other side of me, and I can feel the moment he sits up to look at me too.

"There doesn't need to be some big reaction, but yeah, I do. It's … not a big deal."

A ring of hoots and hollers take place, gaining the attention of other hotel guests, including Nora. She waves from across the pool, and even I crack a smile at how lame we all must look waving to her in sync.

"Way to not draw attention," I say.

"This is huge," Tobias says, grabbing his phone. I yank it from his hand.

"Do not tell Natalie."

"Dude, you know I can't keep secrets from her."

"Oh, so you told her that you watched the new season of *Bridgerton* and then faked all your reactions when you watched it with her later?"

"You said you'd take that to your grave, Quinn!"

"Seriously, you watched *Bridgerton*?" Zane asks.

"It's based off a romance. Of course I watch it. I might write good books, but I've yet to get a movie deal, so I wanted to compare."

"Hold up," Simon says. "Compare the show to the books? As in you've read them all?"

"Fuck. Off. All of you. So, you and Nora, huh?" he asks the guys as they all give their attention back to me.

"I told you, it's nothing."

"Has anything happened?"

Just an almost kiss and a body graze that had me hard as a nail last night, but that is nothing they need to know.

"No. It hasn't."

"You took too long to answer." Beck smiles. "Damn it, I thought I'd be the first to fall for a girl."

"Is it a competition? Because technically, I think I'd win with all the women I see," Zane says.

"You don't count," Beck replies. "I'm talking about good, honest dating. Not living the bachelor life where you use your books, looks, and smooth-talking ways to win a girl for a night."

"Ah, right. I'm out."

"It's not a competition, and I'm serious. Nothing has happened, but if it did, I wouldn't be upset and that's all I'm going to say."

There. End of discussion.

"Dude, you're talking to a group of guys who have based their careers off romance. You have to give us more than that."

Or maybe not.

I shake my head. "Sorry."

"Let's respect his wishes," Tobias says sternly before sitting back on his lounger and looking straight ahead.

"Everything okay?" I ask.

"Fine. Nora is Natalie's best friend, and you're right. It's no one's business but yours and Nora's if something happens."

I nod slowly.

"Thanks," I say just as a flash of red appears in front of us. More precisely, in front of me.

"After all these years, you will always make time for each other, won't you?"

"Yep," Tobias says. "How are you doing today, Nora?"

"I'm good, thank you. Taking a much-needed break like the rest of you."

"Do you want to join us?" Zane asks, elbowing me.

I jerk up from my lounge chair, one foot resting on each side of it. "I'll go find you a seat."

"No need. I'm not staying out long. As much as I want the break, work is always calling."

"Understandable," Zane says too quickly.

I study Nora for a moment. She's always working. In her room, at the signings, on the flights. She needs a break.

"Sit," I tell her and pat my chair.

"No, really, I—"

"Sit," I say again, flashing a big smile.

She nibbles on her bottom lip and nods.

"Have one drink with us, and if you don't have fun, I'll let you go back to your room."

"And if I do have fun?"

"Then you stay here with us and take an entire afternoon off."

"I don't know," she says, flirting. "Could be a bad idea."

"One drink won't hurt you," I say, repeating her words from our last flight.

Her tongue swipes over her lips, and my body inches closer to hers.

"Just one," she says, pulling me out of the trance I'd been falling into.

"Just one," I repeat.

Our focus remains on the other for a moment before someone clears their throat. Nora jolts, and I jerk my head in Zane's direction.

Shit. I'd forgotten they were here.

Pretty sure I just sealed my fate with these guys. I'll never hear the end of it.

CHAPTER NINETEEN

NORA

One drink turned into four, and now I'm in my bathroom getting ready to go out dancing and to get drinks. With six men. Six very attractive men. Especially Hero. Why is he so delicious? And holy shit, does he have a nice body. Hard abs I may have "accidentally" bumped into since we shared a lounge chair and a smooth, sculpted chest that literally screams "touch me." He should wear swim trunks all day, every day.

Damn it. Listen to me. Just thinking about Hero Quinn and … oh my god, I'm going out on the town with *Hero Quinn*. Who am I?

That could be the drinks talking.

Yeah, yeah, all this is totally the drinks talking.

"Whoa, whoa, whoa, what are you doing again? I think the phone cut out because I heard dancing and drinking with the guys."

Pausing mid-application with my eyeshadow, I nod quickly.

"Yup. I said that." I reply, glancing quickly at my phone where I am FaceTiming Natalie. Then I resume my makeup.

"Huh. Remind me again who the guys are?"

"What do you mean, who are they? The guys. You know. Your friends. Hero, Zane, Beck, Graham, Simon, and Tobias."

"Oh." Her eyes widen. "We call them *the guys* now?"

"What else do we call them?"

"I don't know—by their names?"

I huff and wave my mascara. "*The guys* is much more fitting."

My best friend's laugh fills the phone line. "I think I might like this side of you. I'm sad I'm missing it. On the bright side, since Tobias's schedule puts him in Denver with you and Hero, I'm driving down. We should all go out."

"It won't be much fun without all the guys."

"Oh my gosh, stop saying *the guys*." But she's still laughing.

I take another sip of my wine. That's my drink of choice. Moscato, to be exact. "Normally, this wine makes me sleepy, so that's why I chose it, because surely it would do so again and then I'd be back in my room working, but it didn't make me sleepy and now here I am."

"I'm missing out on rambling Nora. I'm so jealous right now."

The screen freezes on my phone.

"Natalie, you there?"

"Yeah, just had to pause to text Tobias."

"Why?"

"To keep an eye on you. Duh."

"You know he will. I already caught him scolding Hero on our way back to our rooms, so he's way ahead of you."

"Why was he scolding Hero?" she asks. The screen freezes again as I finish up with my lipstick.

I shrug. "I'm not sure. I only heard bits and pieces."

"Bits and pieces are enough. Was it about your almost kiss? Oh god, why didn't I think of this?"

The screen freezes again.

"Do not text Tobias about this!"

"Don't you want to know what Hero is thinking without having to ask him?"

She's smart.

"Okay but be cool and don't make it sound like I'm asking."

"On it."

While she does that, I change into one of the dresses I packed. It's nothing fancy. Definitely doesn't scream *let's go clubbing*, but if I add a belt, I can probably maneuver it from knee-length to midthigh, and the straps are changeable, so I'll switch it from both shoulders to just one. I pin my hair up in a messy bun just as Natalie re-appears.

"And?"

"He's not talking, and I quote, *I want to tell you so bad, Natalie, but Hero swore me to secrecy*."

"So they've talked about me?"

I don't need Natalie to tell me my smile is huge. I can feel it.

"Do you want them to?"

"Buzzed Nora does, yes. Sober Nora might be harder to crack."

Someone knocks on my door.

"Oh, they're here. Okay, I'll text you later."

"Have so much fun!"

I hang up, grab my purse, and open the door.

I'd been expecting all the guys to be there, but it's just Hero.

Just Hero, ha. It's *Hero*. Hero standing in the hall in dark wash jeans, a navy dress shirt, and white shoes. His smile reaches ear to ear as he takes me in. I've never dated anyone with facial hair. I bet it tickles when he's doing things that, oh god, I should not be thinking about.

"Wow," he says on a breath. "You look … wow."

I smile and tilt my head. "I can totally see how you write best sellers. Your vocabulary is impeccable."

I pat him on the shoulder and walk right on by.

"Is this how it's going to be?" he asks, following me to the elevator.

"What?"

"You teasing me all the time. I guess I prefer it to ignoring me completely."

I turn to him but don't say a word. The elevator arrives, and we step in.

"Teasing is better than not talking."

"Do you always talk this much when you're nervous?" I ask.

"I'm not nervous. Are you nervous?" He takes a step toward me. His hand reaches out to touch my hip the way he did last night before he left my room.

My body glides toward him as he brings me closer, now resting one hand to cup my cheek and tilt my face to his.

I'm not backing out this time, no way.

But the elevator dings, and just before the doors open, Hero steps back.

The guys are waiting for us, eager to get going.

"Do we have any rules tonight?" Zane asks.

"Just don't miss your flight in the morning," Beck says.

"Perfect."

We follow them out of the hotel entrance, and I'm not even the slightest bit upset that Hero hangs back with me, opens the door for me, and winks at me as soon as we are in the Uber.

A night out with Hero and his friends. Don't mind if I do.

From my point of view, I'm the only woman in this bar slash nightclub with six men.

What am I even doing here? I was full of confidence before, but now I'm all nervous.

"It's pretty loud in here," Simon shouts over the music.

"That's the point," Zane replies.

I'm about to comment that I like this song when a hand snakes around my waist and I'm tugged into a rather solid body.

Hero's to be exact. He hasn't left my side since we got out of the car.

He smells like a sweet spice. Something like cinnamon. I honestly never thought someone could smell so good that I just want to lick them. Yet that's exactly what I want to do to Hero right now.

How many drinks did I have at the pool today?

"The vibe here is off," he says, glancing around.

I'm not sure how he's gathering his information. Smiling faces greet my gaze, and I nod in response.

"The people seem friendly. What don't you like about it?" I ask.

Tobias laughs and Zane snorts.

"I'm getting a drink." Tobias slaps Hero's shoulder. "Do you two want anything?"

"Just a beer," Hero says, and I nod.

"Me too."

"You got it."

He wanders off toward the bartenders, the rest of the group following him. Well, everybody but me and Hero.

"Do you want to go someplace else?" I ask.

He looks down at me with a feisty gaze.

He doesn't say anything, just stares, like he's at war with what he wants to say to me. Then his tongue brushes over his lips. Ah, his mind is going places it shouldn't—and it's taking my mind with it. I wouldn't mind going somewhere else with just him, but that's out of the question. No, that would be the question. There would be a lot of questions.

"Are you two having a conversation or just staring at each other like you want to suck each other's faces off?"

Hero's eyes close at Zane's words, but I just laugh.

"Probably just waiting till later to suck face, I bet."

Ohmygod. Ohmygod. Ohmygod.

Zane's eyes go wide.

Yep, I said it out loud.

"I …" I wave my hand in front of my face. "My throat is dry."

Tobias arrives at that moment and hands me my beer. He hands Hero his as well, and like robots, we both lift them and take a drink. I don't dare look at him after my sip.

"This is going to be a fun night. I can feel it," Zane says.

The rest of the guys return, and we find a table. As soon as we sit, Hero's arm rests behind my seat. There is plenty of room where we are sitting, but his body is flush against mine.

Why do I like this so much?

Hero is supposed to be the one guy I shouldn't want, and yet he's the only guy I can think about right now.

As the night goes on, I'm pretty sure I've figured out why Natalie likes to spend time with these guys so much, and I might have narrowed down how she and Tobias connected. He's funny. He's smart. His comebacks are quick, and Natalie loves a good comeback. He's attractive too. They all are. It's odd, a group of male writers who could all be *GQ* cover models. What are the odds of that? Then again, that's just one girl's perspective. To check my hypothesis, I look to the group of women one table over. Okay, that table is a bad example. They are all staring. Wait? Is that girl glaring at me?

"I'm going to go use the bathroom," I announce and stand. Hero stands immediately.

"I'll walk you."

"To the bathroom?" I ask through a laugh.

"This place is packed, Nora. I want you to be safe."

"I'm a grown woman, Mr. Macho. I'll be fine."

I glance at the group. They are all watching. I take that moment to turn and leave. I can feel Hero hot on my heels.

"I really don't need you to come with me."

"I know you don't," he says, pushing his way through the crowd behind me. "But it wouldn't be right to let you go alone."

"I'm—"

"A grown woman," he snaps as we reach a bit of clearing near the restroom. He grabs my hand. "I know." His eyes roam over my body. "Believe me, I know."

He sucks in a breath, and I swear time stands still as I wait for him to let it out. He moves toward me, his chest bumping into mine, slowly backing me up. My backside meets the wall behind me.

With a hand on each side of my head, Hero leans in. "What are you doing to me?" he whispers.

He closes his eyes as he turns his head ever so slightly toward mine. Our noses touch, and the only sound is our breathing.

"I could ask you the same thing," I reply. The last word is barely off my tongue before his lips crash against mine.

His entire body presses into me as he kisses me hard. I open my mouth to deepen the kiss while his hands slide down my body to cup my ass and lift me. I hang on to him by the neck, holding his lips firmly in line with my own.

"Fuck. I knew you'd taste amazing."

I don't have time to think of a reply before he's kissing me again.

Someone around us whistles, and Hero retreats as if I were on fire as soon as my feet touch the ground.

"I'm … I'm sorry. I'm not sure what came over me," he says. His hands are on his hips as he looks at the ground.

I nod slowly, a finger resting against my lower lip. I'd forgotten where we were, and by the looks of Hero, so did he.

"I … we …" Clearly, he doesn't know what to say.

And to be honest, neither do I. I enjoyed every minute of that with him, and even though he can't form words, I understand him completely.

"Shots?" I ask.

His gaze darts to mine.

"For the table?"

I nod. "Perfect. You get them while I use the ladies' room."

This time, Hero nods. "I'll wait for you."

I raise a brow.

"And repeat what just happened?"

Instead of answering, he steps toward me but stops.

"On second thought, I'll just get the drinks."

My heart is ready to leap from my chest.

"Good idea."

CHAPTER TWENTY

NORA

I should've stayed at the hotel last night.

"This. Is. Rough." I whisper, pulling my sunglasses over my eyes while we sit in our seats as the rest of the passengers board. Hero also has his sunglasses on, and we're both slouched in our seats, heads leaning toward the other, our arms crossed over our travel clothes.

"Yeah, not my best choice," Hero admits with a scratch in his voice. Probably a result of the fact that we are running off only five hours of sleep. This 7:00 a.m. flight showed up fast. Hero did budge a little on his two-hour rule. We arrived at the airport with an hour and twenty minutes before boarding. I appreciated the extra sleep.

And every single one of us made it to the gate on time.

"Nope, it was not."

"But it was fun," he says, slightly lifting his head from the seatback to look at me. Our lips are just inches apart, and thank goodness he can't see my eyes, because that's all I can seem to look at. "And worth it."

The smile that appears on his face is contagious, and the

memory of his lips against mine has been on repeat since the moment it happened.

"Yes, it was."

Nothing scandalous happened while we were out. Not after the kiss, anyway. Not that I didn't want it to. But we were with all his friends and doing anything that remotely indicated something could be happening was asking for a lot of questions neither of us have answers for.

We're headed to Denver for another three-day stop with time off. It's pretty close to home, less than five hours. Will Hero take this time to drive back to Wind Valley after tomorrow's signing? I prefer vacations by the hotel pool, sitting shoulder to shoulder with Hero, lying in the sun and listening to his buddies tease him.

I learned a lot by that pool in Dallas yesterday.

Hero played soccer in high school. He had one girlfriend until graduation but hasn't dated anyone serious since they broke up. I could have sworn he dated in college, but as they said, it was nothing serious. He's broken both his wrists, which to his surprise, do not bother him when he sits to write for hours, and he believed in the Easter Bunny far too long. His words.

They aren't big things to know about someone, but the more I get to know Hero, the more I think that had he made it to the table the night of our date, our present could be very different right now. Heck, we could be married with kids. Maybe he wouldn't have blasted away with words and become a best seller, and maybe I wouldn't have my business. I love my business.

I probably would have enjoyed this daydream life, but things happen for a reason. Perhaps Hero not showing up was the driving force I needed to get my butt in gear. It was only a month after that I decided what I wanted to do, and that was because I had ruled men out once he stood me up. Perhaps I have Hero to thank for my career.

I glance over at him. He's removed his sunglasses and is now sitting up a little straighter as he rubs the spot between his eyes.

"Can I get a cup of coffee and a bottle of water when you have a moment, please?" he asks the flight attendant. She nods. "Make it two of each. I think my friend will need one too."

His friend. Ha. I smile because it's true, but I'm not sure how we got here. It just sort of happened, and now, I'm pretty sure we are already skating past that line.

"Of course. Would you like cream?"

"Just black," Hero and I answer in unison.

The three of us let out a small laugh as the flight attendant gets back to work.

"Thanks. She may as well bring a pitcher because I'm going to need it," I say.

"Me too. I'd say I was going straight to the hotel to sleep when we get there, but I'm just—"

"Not a nap person?" I finish for him.

"Nope."

"Me either. I'll probably even stay up till like ten tonight and then wake up tomorrow at the same time I always do, a ripe 5:30 a.m., and feel refreshed."

He chuckles, and oh my god, why do I enjoy it so much?

"If I nap, my whole day will be thrown off and I'll feel like I wasted it. I'm just thankful that both the signing and my date aren't until tomorrow."

His date. Right. The ones I set up for him with other women.

So that I could move on and not think of him that way.

Is that still what I want?

You're here to find him a girlfriend, and you can't forget that.

No matter what my feelings are, this survey has a purpose. Whether it is for my reasons or for him to keep his career on track, there is no turning back.

"What do you plan on doing with your free day if you don't

plan on napping?" Hero asks, taking his coffee. Next, he pops the top off his water and starts to chug.

"I'm not sure yet. I have some emails to catch up on. Maybe even write a proposal for another new client and then—"

"You're going to spend it working. What a surprise."

I twist the cap off my own bottle to stay busy. "I like to get ahead."

"So do I, but I also know that taking a day off every so often is smart." He taps his temple. "Let the brain relax and regroup from time to time."

"Sure," I say and sip my coffee. "What do you call yesterday or last night?"

He grins.

Lord help me. Why is this a thing for me now? He smiles. So what? Everyone smiles. It's not like he does it better than most.

"I definitely do not call it relaxing my brain. The pool afternoon, sure, but last night? Last night was a surprise. I need a real break. I need water and greasy food and something normal."

Having greasy food is normal for him? Doubt it.

Hero studies me as I take another sip. It's unsettling. Am I drinking funny? Spilling coffee on myself?

I glance down quickly, but there is no mess.

Why am I like this under his gaze?

"Why don't you come hang out with me today?" he asks.

"With you?" I ask through a laugh. "Oh, you're serious?" I backtrack at the sour expression on his face.

"I won't force you."

"I didn't mean it like that." My hand instinctively rests on his forearm. "I meant like, aren't you sick of me by now? We just spent an entire day together."

And we kissed last night and neither of us has yet to bring it up. Are we just going to keep hanging out and pretend that it didn't happen?

"You're kidding, right?"

I shake my head.

"Nora, we have hung out every single day since this tour started. How will this be any different?"

I shrug. "Because it's not for work."

"Last night wasn't for work and it went just fine. So what do you say? Do you think we can survive another day together?"

Probably. And yet, he mentioned last night and not the kiss.

"Sure. Why not?" I finally remove my sunglasses and eye him suspiciously. He's already thinking of something. "What did you have in mind?"

"A baseball game. The weather is going to be nice when we get there, the wind minimal, and I could use a hot dog, some popcorn, and a cold beer."

A baseball game. That actually sounds fun. I can't even remember the last time I went to one. I'll be the first to admit that I put work before almost everything, so events like this are always on the back burner.

"It's not the worst idea," is what I say to Hero instead.

"Jesus, can you two stop talking already?" A voice chimes in from the crack between our seats. "I have a day planned with Natalie after we land, and I need to sleep this entire flight, but I can't do it with the two of you jibber jabbering the entire time."

Hero and I share a gaze as we hold back our laughter. I'd almost forgotten Tobias was on the plane with us.

"Jibber jabber?" I mouth to Hero.

He leans in. "See, this day is going to be great. You'll see."

* * *

The man in front of me stops abruptly and steps back, smashing the hot dog in my hand into my chest.

Noooo.

"What part of the day is this supposed to be good?" I ask, peeling my afternoon snack off my shirt and dropping it into the trash. First, the landing into Denver was bumpy, and I almost threw up, then my bag was the last one off the conveyor—we actually thought it didn't make it, and Hero wasn't shy about reminding me of his two-hour boarding rule—and then the Uber driver got lost on his way to airport pickup and charged us because he never found us. So by the time we made it to the hotel, we had about an hour before the game, which was fine because Coors Field is in walking distance. But this is just the cake topper.

"What's that? Oh shoot, I almost ran into you with my hot—what happened?" Hero asks, his eyes glued to where the ketchup stain has now spread from my horrible job of wiping it up with a napkin. The stain just so happens to sit perfectly over my right breast.

"I ran into the guy in front of me," I tell him just as someone bumps his shoulder. His food remains untouched in his hand, but our shoulders knock together. I can't think of a point in this day when we haven't been touching.

Hero looks around. "I didn't expect this many people to be here today. For some reason, I thought Friday day games would be slower."

"Not this one. I'm going to duck into the restroom to see if I can clean this up a bit more. Meet you at our seats?"

He nods. "I'll just wait for you outside the bathroom."

"Oh boy, this again? That's not necessary."

"This place is packed, Nora."

"Exactly. I'll be fine."

His gaze holds mine and when he can finally see that I'm not going to budge, he nods.

"Ten minutes, tops," I tell him and head for the closest restroom.

Once I'm inside, I take a breath and stare at my reflection. God, Natalie would die if she knew I was willingly hanging out one-on-one with Hero for something other than business purposes again. Shoot, I swore to myself that night he stood me up that I would never, ever give this man the time of day, and yet here I am, years later, doing just that. And liking it. I like it a lot.

Maybe this is good. I'm not a fan of holding a grudge, and something was bound to happen sooner or later to mend this rift between us, right?

Turns out, all it took was an open schedule and a bad review to get us together. Oh, and poor planning on my cousin's part. I've heard of tours that have multiple stops with days in between, but this every other day stuff is crazy. There is a lot more free time on these things than I thought.

As if she knew I was thinking of her, a text comes through from Natalie.

Natalie: How's the date?

Nora: It's not a date. How do you even know where I am?

Natalie: Tobias told me. He's mad that you didn't invite us to join you.

Nora: He said he had plans with you. I assumed he already had something in the books.

Natalie: Watching you and Hero together would have been so much more fun.

Nora: We're just friends.

Natalie: Friends?! I'm soooo coming to your room later so you can tell me all about this.

Nora: I have to go.

Natalie: Boo. Fine. Have fun!

. . .

I debate telling her about the kiss but decide not to. If we are pretending it never happened, there isn't a reason to get her all worked up.

I stuff my phone into my crossbody bag, grab a handful of paper towels, and get to work on my shirt. It doesn't take long to come to the conclusion that my shirt is ruined and white is not a shirt you should ever wear to a baseball game.

Sadly, there are no automatic dryers here, so a wet shirt with a red stain over my boob will have to be my style for today.

At least it's not my pants. I can handle this.

God, if this were a real date, I would be mortified, but it's not, so for that I am truly thankful.

I spot Hero outside of the bathroom immediately. He's right across from the exit, holding his food, drink, and a bag with the Rockies logo all over it, so it's a no-brainer that it came from the pro shop.

"Supporting the team?" I ask. I almost went with a sassy comment about how he waited for me when I told him not to, but we still have a few more hours together. Although I'm pretty sure he now interprets my sass as flirting, so I'm in uncharted territory at this point.

His grin is wide and charming. "I got you a new shirt. I hope that's okay."

He … he bought me a shirt? That's actually pretty sweet.

I could easily just go the rest of the day with the one I have, spot and all, but it is wet and there is a breeze, so … I reach for the bag.

"Thank you, Hero. I'll be right back."

"I'll be right here."

I don't even attempt to argue this time. Instead, I change quickly and pop back out, ready to find our seats.

"The black was a good choice," I say and point to the shirt. It's a simple T-shirt, soft like those vintage tees, and so comfortable. When I opened the bag, I was certain he got me a vee neck shirt because everyone assumes that's the style women like, but not me. I like an old- fashioned T-shirt, and clearly, Hero has noticed.

"I thought so too. Come on. Our seats are this way."

I follow behind him, but the crowd is thick. Hero effortlessly reaches for my hand. It's not just your simple handhold either. It's full on, fingers laced together, tugging my arm until my front is flush with his back hand-holding.

"I don't want to lose you in the crowd," he says over his shoulder.

My shoulders drop. I knew that was why he did it, but my body tried to betray me into hoping this meant something else. Which is crazy. Hero and I aren't like that. Not even in the slightest way. Despite the kiss last night.

When we get to our row and the amount of people around us has dwindled by a lot, my heart doesn't skip a beat to remind my brain that we are still holding hands. In fact, he doesn't even let go of my hand once we are seated.

The worst part: nothing in me has the urge to pull away from him. Even though I know I'm going to fully overanalyze this later and probably even scold myself for not stopping it, I'm going to enjoy every last moment of him touching me.

"Here," he says and hands me his hotdog. "I'll grab another one when the away team gets up to bat."

"Oh no, it's fine. I can go."

"Take it, Nora. It's just a hot dog, and even if you don't take it, I'll still be the one to get you something to eat, so either you take this one or we both sit here and let it get cold."

I crack a smile and take the food. "Only you would tell a girl what to do with something as boring as a hot dog."

He chuckles. "Yeah, I was pretty demanding, wasn't I?"

"You were, but I'll take it because I'm hungry. However, let the record show that I am a grown woman who is fully capable of getting her own hot dog."

"Noted, and please let the record show that it is also perfectly okay to let a man spoil you," he says as I take a giant bite. I swipe my tongue over my lips to catch the excess mustard. Hero is watching me, so I sit back to watch the game.

Then I take a deep breath. I hadn't meant for my tongue swipe to be sexy, but with the way Hero was just looking at me, it was more than innocent.

I sneak a glance, and this time Hero is sitting ramrod straight with his hands on his knees.

"I'll just go get that food right now," he says and stands. "Do you want anything else?"

"No thanks," I answer as he walks off.

Good. A little space is good.

The lineup goes through a couple of batters, nothing super exciting to report, when a body drops into the seat next to me.

"You didn't miss much," I say, leaning in only to jump back as soon as I turn my head and see that it's not Hero sitting next to me.

It's a random man I have never seen before in my life.

"Sorry, I didn't mean to scare you. I just thought I'd come say hey while your friend is away."

Think fast. Think fast, Nora. How can I get him to go away? I could tell him the truth, but the look in his eyes is definitely giving off "I'm not that easy to get rid of" vibes. How do I do this with the least amount of confrontation?

"Oh, you mean my boyfriend."

That's perfect.

"Huh, I didn't sense that when I saw you two sitting here."

"We are dating." I nod. "Me and him. Him being Hero. That's his name. Hero. We have been together for years."

I look toward the field as I talk. *Focus on the game and he will get the hint.* Conversation over and situation resolved.

"Well, he's not a bright man to leave someone so pretty sitting all alone."

Shitballs.

"Ah yes, well—"

"Can I help you?" Hero's voice is firm and demanding. It startles me at first but also turns me on a little.

The guy sitting in Hero's seat looks up slowly. "Nope."

My eyes flash to Hero's. I assume he'd be glaring at the man in his seat, but he isn't. He's watching me. "You okay?" he mouths. I shrug and then nod.

I mean, the guy is just trying to flirt and clearly can't take a hint, but he isn't hurting anyone.

"Well, you can help me by getting out of my seat," Hero says. "Now."

The guy lets out a long sigh but stands. "Sure thing."

As soon as this guy and Hero are standing chest to chest, warning bells go off in my head. Hero barely takes a step for his seat when the other guy retreats.

That's good. This is over and now we can watch the game.

"How long was he sitting here?"

"Not long," I answer.

"Are you okay?" He reaches for my chin to gently force me to look at him.

"Yes."

"Positive?" he asks again.

"I'm positive, Hero."

His eyes search mine as if they were looking for the real answer. He must not find what he's searching for because he nods, begins to eat his hot dog, and watches the game.

That's the most exciting the game gets. Well, unless you count the fact that as soon as he finished eating, his arm went to the back on my chair and occasionally his thumb brushes my shoulder, causing my brain to short-circuit and my heart to race while I forget that I'm supposed to be watching a baseball game.

Damn it.

This wasn't supposed to happen, and I'm not supposed to wish he'd kiss me again.

CHAPTER TWENTY-ONE

HERO

I'm not a possessive man.

I've never thought of myself as the type to feel the need to shout from rooftops that something belongs to me, but yesterday … yesterday was different.

When I'd returned to my seat at the baseball game to find some guy sitting there talking to Nora, I wanted to haul him up and toss him into the field. That was my seat, and that was my girl.

Except she wasn't. Isn't. Fuck.

Is that what it's like for her when I'm on a date? She couldn't have been sitting with that guy for longer than five minutes, but still, seeing her with another man … I hated it.

Holding her hand was where I went wrong. Or maybe it was inviting her to spend the day with me, or maybe it even started yesterday at the pool.

The pool? Right. It was the kiss last night. The fucking epic kiss that my brain won't let me forget about. Kissing her was better than I imagined it would be.

But holding her hand and knowing that I was doing it to keep her close to me—that was different.

As soon as I locked her hand in mine, it felt right. I knew that holding her hand wasn't going to be enough. Then she licked that mustard off her lip, and I was gone.

The home team wasn't the only one thinking of how to get on base.

All the feelings from college came flooding in. I knew they were there, creeping in. I admitted as much earlier, but now I know for sure that everything I ever felt for Nora never actually went away. It only faded into the background, waiting for its moment to reappear. And boy, did it. My palms were sweating.

"Are you all set?" Nora asks.

I look up from my table, where books and books of my words are stacked next to me. Most readers already have a copy to bring, but some like to buy new copies just to have a special edition with my signature in it.

"I'm ready," I tell her. When am I ever not ready?

If someone had told me that I would be a popular romance writer when I grew up, I'd have full-blown snorted in their faces.

I was determined to be a football player or a soccer player or anything with sports. Writing was just something I did for fun at night. Once I had my first girlfriend though, romance writing was a habit.

Nora walks away from me. She wears dress pants and a blouse almost every day, and today is no different. Except it is. Today I notice the sway of her hips. The way she brushes her hair over shoulder. How she smiles through her eyes when she talks to people. How she smells and smiles and types something into her phone.

I know I have to go on these dates, but I'll be counting down the minutes till I'm alone with Nora. Not that I'd do anything about it … again. I just want to be near her and get to know her.

Her comfort level with me has visibly changed, and she no longer talks to me as if I'm the last person she'd be caught conversing with. I'd go as far as to say she's friendly. Sometimes even more than friendly.

And boy, oh boy, do I want to be more than friendly with her.

She's my unicorn. We spent years apart from each other, yet with each moment I'm with her, even when she's putting me through hell, I still want to be with her.

I really wish I knew what was going on inside her mind.

Readers start to pile in, so I get to work mingling and taking pictures with them. I'm thankful for the number of people who show up to these things for me, especially despite recent events in my career.

All I can do is take one day at a time and let Nora work her magic.

As if she knows I'm thinking of her, she moves toward me, bending at the hip to whisper in my ear, "Enjoy your date tonight."

She moves away just as quickly, but I reach for her hand and pull her back gently.

"See you after?" I ask, meeting her gaze. She takes a deep breath, recovering quickly with a cheeky grin.

"If you're lucky."

* * *

"So you'd rather read a romantic suspense than a romantic comedy?" I ask my date, Tina, and then laugh at the guilty expression on her face.

"Don't get me wrong. I love your books, but if it were a life-or-death situation and I had to choose, romantic suspense is the way to go."

I shake my head. "Cozy mystery?"

"Only if it's sweet. I like to leave the heat to everything else."

"Huh."

"I think it's normal to like all genres of romance."

"So do I, but I've assumed that if a reader enjoyed steamy books, the sweet ones would bore then."

"It's all about the story," Tina says and then smiles at the waitress when she drops off our food. I ordered the chicken and she the mahi.

"I have to say, tonight has been pleasant."

She chews quickly and then asks, "Have the other dates not been?"

"They haven't been this laidback and easy."

"Easy, I'm anything but." Tina winks and I let out a chuckle.

"That's exactly what I mean."

"So, tell me, does that woman who came to get our picture earlier follow you on every date?" Tina nods in a direction over my shoulder, and I twist to see Nora. She isn't paying attention to us, but she's still here. Usually, she's gone by the time dinner comes out, so what is different about tonight?

I have the urge to excuse myself to ask her, but I'm here for a date. A date Nora set me up on. No matter what happened between us, one thing is certain: Nora still thinks I can find love on this tour. and I get the feeling she doesn't want it to be her.

I found every reason to touch her at the game yesterday, to let her know where my mind is, and the way she didn't respond or even notice tells me we aren't on the same page and the other night was simply just the drinks.

Talk about an ego blow.

"She collects pictures and documents different things so I can focus on my date."

"Oh, I never thought of it like that. That's sweet of her."

It would be sweeter if she shared the feelings I did.

"It's her job." I shrug. "Tell me more about you."

"I—"

Her hand goes to throat, her eyes widen, and then she covers mouth.

I am a trooper. I don't get grossed out very easily. My niece even pooped on me once. I pulled the diaper back and that green mush went right under my fingernail. I didn't flinch.

I also didn't flinch when Tommy Mintley broke his leg in fifth grade, the bone sticking right out and blood everywhere. But I also remember getting this weird feeling right before it happened. Like I needed to brace myself for something bad.

Right now, that feeling is back.

Tina smiles for the briefest of moments before vomit spews from her mouth all over the table, some of it washing over my dinner and spilling into my lap.

She heaves once, twice, three times before looking up.

"Oh god," she groans.

I remain completely still as she scoots her chair back. "I'm going to run to the restroom. I'm so, so, sorry."

I wave a hand and close my eyes. "I'll get you some water as soon as I get myself cleaned up."

I grab a couple of the paper napkins and clean up as much vomit as I can before retreating to the bathroom, where I basically soak my crotch in water before I return to the table.

I take my seat and sip my drink.

"Sir," the waitress says as soon as I put my glass down.

I look up.

"The woman you were with asked me to pass on a message."

Technically, I was with Nora at one point before Tina, so I'm not too sure who she's referring to.

"She said, *your books are amazing and I'm sorry I puked and ran. Have a good night.*"

Ah, Tina.

"Thanks."

"So, the check?"

I nod. "Actually, can you add two slices of cheesecake to the check first? I'll take them to go."

"Of course."

I look to where I'd spotted Nora earlier. She's not here anymore.

It's probably a good thing she didn't record the last few minutes. I'm not so sure what kind of light this will shine on me.

I'll see what she thinks when I get back to the hotel.

The waitress returns quickly with the check and two boxes.

I sign the ticket and stare at the white Styrofoam.

I'm leaving the date with one woman to go see a different one who doesn't like me the way I like her, but I'm bringing her dessert anyway.

I've officially lost all control over my life.

And yet, even if she doesn't want me like that, I have to see her again. Tonight.

CHAPTER TWENTY-TWO

NORA

This is wrong. So, so wrong.

I feel like I'm doing something illegal. Setting Hero up on these dates and then waiting for him to come back to me. To which he's only coming back to my room to update me so that I can update his social media. You know, because I'm his marketing manager.

You know what? Not tonight. Not in my room. We are professionals. We should be meeting in the public eye. I need to keep this professional.

He made her laugh a lot tonight.

His date, that is.

So much laughing.

It looked like he was having fun, and the photos I took of him smiling have already received more than a few thousand likes.

I only posted it early because … well … I don't know. It definitely wasn't because I wanted anyone to see where he was and interrupt their *fun* date.

Nope.

I should be happy, right?

My plan to get him a girlfriend is working.

I grab my computer and phone and head toward the lobby and hotel bar and ask for a large glass of wine.

I find an open spot and prop open my computer as I take the first sip.

The whole point of these dates is so that he finds love, right? Would it be so wrong if he found it, even if not on the actual dates themselves?

Okay, put the wine down.

I set my glass down and shake my head. I'm about to be weeks ahead of work, so I should put my head down and enjoy how organized I am. Not think of a man who is literally out with another woman right this second.

And it works. For about ten seconds.

She was pretty too. And kind. Ugh. I bet they hit it off.

Hero and I have done nothing but hang out and hold hands and kiss. Once. Just once. We don't even have any heavy breathing happening. Nope, just me with these thoughts in my head. Okay, so maybe a little heavy breathing. On my part anyway.

But a woman doesn't just make this stuff up in her mind. A man, in my case Hero, has to have done something to make me think there is something more.

Two white boxes plop on the table next to my laptop.

"Bad night?" Hero asks.

I fail to hide my smile as I spin in my stool to face him. "It's been—oh my god what happened?" I ask, taking in his appearance. Then I look at the clock. "Wait, I left the restaurant not thirty minutes ago, how are you back already?"

"I'm not exactly sure. Tina suddenly got sick, threw up on the table, and then bolted. Left a note with the waiter that she was leaving."

"What?" Even though it's not funny, I laugh. "You made that up."

"Honestly, I wish I had."

"Tell me the truth," I say and shove his arm.

"That is the truth." He takes the seat next to me as the bartender comes up. "Just a water, please." Hero's head hangs in defeat.

"These dates have not been what I was expecting."

"Wait, hold that thought," I tell him and get my phone out. "Let's record this. We haven't done any postdate video updates, so this would be great right now."

He sighs and then nods. "We have to keep the momentum going, right? Can't let anyone down."

The sadness in his voice makes me want to change my mind on a video, but he's right about the momentum. We can't stop now.

I hold up my phone and hit record.

"So, Hero, you've been on three official dates this far. What are you thinking?"

He runs a hand over his face and then smiles into the camera.

"I think that interacting with my readers has been amazing, and even if it's not a dating survey each year, I need to plan something more fun that just signing books and taking pictures with them."

"Aw, that's sweet, but tell us about the dates. Any favorites yet?"

Okay, okay, I'm fishing. I'm a woman and I have feelings, so sue me.

His head cocks to the side before he answers. "Tonight was a good night, before things took a turn for the worst. In fact, I think a do-over would be great. Plus, I'd like to know that she's okay and …"

The rest of his sentence blurs in my head. He wants to go on a second date with Tina. The woman he made laugh and who smiled at him like he was this rare gem she'd never seen before.

Wow.

"Nora." Hero waves a hand in my face." Did you hear me?"

"Huh?" I say and end the video. "Oh yeah, yeah, you want me to reach out to Tina for another date."

I can't wait.

"Just coffee or lunch is fine, but I was referring to what I asked you after that. About my room."

Shit, I have no clue.

"Fine. I'll just take this." He grabs the to-go boxes. "And eat these slices of cheesecake in my room."

"Cheesecake?" I sit up quickly, easing into a stand.

He nods. "With chocolate sauce on the side."

All right, so we have established that I know next to nothing about adult Hero Quinn, but it's now officially clear as day that I judged college Hero Quinn way too harshly. The only way this man right here would know that cheesecake with a side of chocolate sauce is my favorite is if he paid attention on Friday nights when I'd tag along with Natalie when she hung out with Tobias and his friends.

And now Hero has cheesecake. Two slices to be exact, and that means he intentionally brought one back to the hotel for me.

A shirt and now cheesecake.

Don't overthink it. Friends do this stuff all the time and now we are friends.

Friends.

"Are you okay?" Hero asks, reclaiming his seat to look me in the eyes.

"I'm fine."

He narrows his gaze, his focus all on me. Do I have a tell when I lie? I'm not trying to lie right now. I honestly do think his date will go well, but I also thought this date would go well too.

"Okay," he says and stands. "But I'm still taking this." He grabs both boxes. "You really do work too hard. Let's take a break."

He tosses some cash onto the bar and closes my computer.

"For someone who releases like five books a year, you're one to talk—and how is that possible with the schedule you have?"

He shrugs. "My schedule on tour versus at home are nowhere near the same, and this tour is definitely not like my others."

"I believe it."

"Come on, Nora, come watch TV with me."

"What if you go get your computer and we work together instead? I mean, you'll do your work, and I'll do mine."

He thinks about it for a moment but shakes his head. "Maybe next time, but a break is good for me from time to time, and tours seem to be when I take my break. Come. Watch. TV."

"I'm working."

I try to open my computer again, but Hero grabs it and starts walking toward the elevator.

"Come watch TV or let's go to a club. Those are your options."

"Why are those my only two options?" I grab my glass quickly, since I wasn't finished, and follow behind him.

Although I did have fun clubbing with him a couple nights ago. Maybe I should indulge a little.

"Because those are the options you get."

I sigh. Both options include Hero and I hanging out, so I may as well take the one with a lot less work. And the one that includes me eating cheesecake in bed.

"Just this one night. Okay?"

"Yes!" He claps and then nods at the buttons on the elevator, and I press the one for our floor.

As soon as we are in his room, his scent surrounds me. I don't move from the doorway.

He sits on one side of the bed and pats the other.

I climb onto the bed beside him, and his grin widens.

“Why are you being weird?” I ask.

“I’m not.” He chuckles. “I’m just happy is all.”

Oh dear lord. I hate to admit this, but if complying to his request warrants that reaction every time, I very well may never say no to this man.

I settle in on my side, pulling my knees up and letting them fall to the side. As soon as I do this simple, *simple* action, Hero shifts on the bed and now my knees are draped over his thighs. On instinct, I move to readjust, but his arms shoot out, resting over my legs while his to-go box balances in his lap. I open my box and look at the delicious dessert.

I should be devouring this, but my heart is racing, and it doesn't take a rocket scientist to know that I will not be watching any of whatever is on the TV. Nor will I enjoy this snack the way it should be enjoyed. My mind is now focused on Hero and the fact that we are touching. Not just touching, but one butt scoot away from cuddling together on a bed. Alone in a hotel room. Where we are adults and can do anything we want.

I want way more than I should be thinking right now.

Oh god. I’m falling for Hero, and there isn’t anything I can do to stop it.

I’m not sure how much time passes, but it’s enough that both cheesecakes are gone, and I fell asleep while watching TV.

As I stir to turn the television off and get comfortable, I notice that it was enough time for Hero to fall asleep as well.

His hair looks soft and smooth as he lay curled up against the pillow. His facial features, so defined and firm when he looks at me, seem gentler now. He’s got a scar I never noticed before on his left cheek. I lean in closer to see if there is anything else I've missed. Damn, he smells good. Even after a long day he still smells like lemons and spice.

He'd kicked his shoes off, and for some reason that makes me feel like our relationship has hit a new level.

I should wake him.

Falling for Hero Quinn would end in nothing but heartache. I've been through it once, can I do it again?

I'll enjoy this for tonight, but tomorrow—tomorrow he goes on a second date with Tina and then on another date in the evening, per our survey schedule.

He's going to find the perfect woman for him on this tour.

That's the best choice right now.

CHAPTER TWENTY-THREE

HERO

I went to bed with Nora next to me and woke up alone.

I wanted her to be here when I woke up. I really did. After all, not only did I wake up in the middle of the night to her face, but our legs were tangled, our arms were tangled as well. Shoot, I have no doubt that she woke up and freaked out that we were wrapped up in each other's limbs.

I rub a hand over my face.

I can't read her. She might not be overly affectionate physically to me, but damn, when we are together, everything just feels … easy. Right. She has to feel it, too, doesn't she?

Damn.

I like her. A lot. I need to tell her.

But how am I going to tell her? She didn't come down for breakfast, and when I texted her back about my follow-up lunch with Tina, she just said that she would see me at the signing.

Well, I'm here now and she isn't. Which could be a good thing. If Nora wants details on my lunch with Tina, she won't get much. Tina, although touched I reached out and wanted to make sure she was okay, doesn't think we are a match. I almost laughed when she said it. I didn't think we were either, and I didn't think inviting her to lunch to see how she was feeling really hinted "let's date again," but I can see how it might be perceived that way. Either way, lunch was short. It's probably for the best since I thought of Nora the entire time.

And how I'm dying to kiss her again.

"Hey, man," Beck slaps a hand on my shoulder. "How's the tour?"

"Hey," I say, moving to shake his hand. "I didn't know you were going to be here today."

"Yeah, a couple of the stops on my tour got switched up. This is my last one though. I only had five stops compared to your seven."

"Yeah, it's a longer tour for me, that's for sure."

He nods toward the room where readers are beginning to gather. "What are you signed up for today?"

"A reading, it seems," I say, taking in the setup of the room.

"From what book?"

"No clue. I'll find out when I get there."

Beck shakes his head. "I'd need to know ahead of time to practice reading it."

Doug asked me if I wanted to either pick the book or the scene, but I told him that it didn't matter. Honestly, I think he said he was going to let the owner of the bookstore pick. Either way, I don't need much prep time. Reading in front of strangers doesn't bother me.

"I'm not too worried."

"Well, good luck to you. And see you in a couple weeks? I love meeting all these readers, but I miss our weekly writing sessions more."

"Tell me about it. My mind has too much going on to focus. I've had a few successful writing moments to myself, but not as many as I want."

The opportunities are there every night, but I clearly find other things to fill my time.

"Ah, right, the marketing manager." His brows dance as he smiles. "How are things going with Nora?"

I sigh.

"It's complicated, but I like her. I just need to figure out what to do about it."

"I'm sure you will. You write novels that legitimately create and solve situations like this all the time. You'll figure it out."

"I wish it were that easy. Honestly, at this point, I just need to tell her how I feel."

"So, it can be that easy, then?"

"Till I think about her saying it's one-sided."

"Oh."

The way he said it, all surprised and thrown off, alarms me. """What does *oh* mean?"

"I just … I didn't think you'd ever be nervous to admit your feelings to anyone. You're a very blunt person."

I nod. "This is different."

"Well," he clamps a hand down on my shoulder, "different is good. That's how you know it's real. I don't think she will turn you down. When will you tell her?"

I think for a moment. "Tonight."

I have to. It doesn't do me any good wondering all the time, and if I just know how she feels, I can get my head back in the game with these survey dates. Get my eye back on the author of the year prize. Author of the year with the girl of his dreams by his side.

Yeah, I'll take my chances.

"After this reading?"

I shake my head and cringe. "After my date."

"Oh." This time it's more of a *yikes* oh.

"Tell me about it."

Going on another date when the only woman I want is Nora really sucks.

"Well, good luck and let me know how it goes."

* * *

A few readers cheer when I enter the room, and I wave like normal. There is a chair set up for me with rows and rows of readers in the audience. I spot Nora in the back and smile. I let out a breath. I'm growing too accustomed to having her here. On tour. Having someone to go back to at night and just be with.

If she doesn't feel the same, any tour from here on out is going to suck.

"How is everyone tonight?" I ask, taking my seat and looking at the mic. It's like I'm about to put on a concert. I'm not on a stage or anything, but there are enough people here that I clearly need a mic for them all to hear me.

"Denver is one of my favorite places to visit. It's close to home, and I feel like I have more in common with my readers when we are this close. So, I better get a picture to remember you all. Nora, will you come grab one for me to put online?"

She joins me immediately, then waits for me to kneel with the audience for a picture.

She snaps it and then hands me the book with the pages marked to read.

As soon as I see the cover, I start to sweat.

It's my very first novel. I've written dozens since this one, and this is the one the bookstore picked. I swear I thought they'd pick my newest release. It's what we normally do.

Shit.

I've never been so nervous about my writing. Yeah, in my mind, I had assumed Nora had read my books and maybe even read this part of this particular book, but I was never certain. If she had, the moment in *the* scene clearly didn't stand out as much to her as it did to me.

My gaze flicks to hers for the smallest moment before I clear my throat.

It's damn hot in here.

I let out a breath and then wink at the crowd as I begin.

I have to hold it together. What are the chances that the scene chosen is even that scene?

I flip the book open.

High. The chances are fucking high.

I take a deep breath and then begin to read. This is my job after all, and I can't let them down.

As the Uber driver drove me to dinner, I thought of the first night I met her. I didn't want to go to a party that night. I wanted to stay at home and keep working. I was so close to finishing another book that doing anything else felt wrong. But my friends convinced me that I needed a break, and they were right. I was on my second beer when she walked in the room. She wore a red maxi dress, as my sister called them, and her hair was pinned up in a bun. She wasn't smiling. She looked annoyed and I wondered if my face looked like that because I was pretty sure this girl knew how I felt. Then she looked at me. We ended the night talking for hours about nothing and everything, and I asked her on a date.

The exact date I'm headed to now.

I walked into the restaurant, running late because I lost track of time while writing, again. And there she was sitting cross-legged in a corner booth in a bright blue dress and playing with her hair—which was beautiful, by the way—and she was smiling at the waiter as he talked.

She was talking to him so effortlessly—how I hoped that was the way it was when she talked to me. I had only one night to compare it to, but I prayed that we would have those moments for as long as she would let me.

I was about to step up to the table when my phone buzzed. I shouldn't have looked at it. I should have ignored it, but I didn't.

I pulled it from my pocket and saw the name of a friend who was working his way up as a literary agent. He was new to the field, and I'd met him the semester just before he graduated.

"Hello?" I answered.

I pause and it takes everything in my power not to look at Nora.

I go on.

"Hey! Glad I caught you. Look, I know this is crazy, but I was just talking to the owner of Hook'em Books—can you believe it? Holy shit! I was telling him about your writing group, and he thinks I'm lying to him, that I made you all up. Do you have a manuscript you can send me right now? Anything will do. Something for proof. He said if I can get a manuscript in the next thirty minutes, he'll sign you, manuscript unread. It will be your first book deal, dude. How crazy is this? This is the luck of the draw, I swear."

Shit, I never realized how spot on the details were with my real life. With our past, she's sure to know it's about her.

I swallow and flip to the next page. The page with exactly why I never made it to the table. With what I couldn't find it in myself to tell Nora. It's not like some devastating story. At that moment, I thought I was making the right choice. But now, it seems foolish. It's embarrassing that I wasn't older, wiser, or even braver to just admit I could have done things different.

I go on with the scene.

"Are you kidding me?" I asked him. "You're messing with me, aren't you?"

But it sounded like he just got me a book deal without even giving them a book—if I get it to him right now. I bet this was a test of what kind of client I would be.

"I'm not kidding. Send it to me right now. Are you at your computer?"

"No I'm ..." My words trailed off.

My date was still playing with her hair, but now she was focused on her phone. Probably checking the time, because every moment I stood here, I was later and later.

"Dude, please tell me you're about to press send. This could be it. The big break. Take this chance with me, man. This could be the start to an amazing career. What could be more important than that?"

I slowly took a step back. The dream job or the girl I just met.

I kept my eyes on my date. If, for even one second, I thought my career was more important than the girl waiting for me alone at a table, she deserved better. She deserved a man who was going to put her first. I clearly wasn't that man.

"Give me five minutes," I said and left the restaurant.

As soon as I'd hit send a few minutes later, I was thankful that I'd picked a restaurant so close to where I lived. I remember thinking that this could very well turn out to be the best night of my life. I was at a stage in my life where I needed to put career first and relationships last. So, I went to a party and made out with some chick.

A week later, when my buddy came through and I was offered my first contract, I wanted to call her. *I wanted to share it with* her, *but I was too late. I'd just lost my unicorn.*

Now, though, I have a chance to prove to a woman that I am worthy, and this is my story.

A reader in the crowd begins to clap immediately and many follow suit. Me, I stare at the words. The story that followed the prologue of my first book had nothing to do with Nora. It was about a man who used the guilt he felt on that night to make him a better person once he had the chance to date again. Inspired by Nora, yes, Written about her, no.

I look toward the back to where Nora had been standing, but she's gone.

Shit.

CHAPTER TWENTY-FOUR

NORA

Holy shit.

Holy shit.

Holy. Shit.

That was me. Oh my god. He wrote a book about me. Me. Nora Grayson, and he called me his unicorn. Holy mother of … what is happening?

My knee bounces under the steakhouse's table as I glance up at Hero. He's a couple tables over, waiting for his date, who, by the way, is almost half an hour late.

I need to talk to him, but right now is clearly not the time. Of course he's on a date. That would be just my luck. For him to finally reveal what happened on that night and then to go out with another woman.

Yet I'm the reason he's out on a date with said woman.

How is this my life right now?

"Can I sit down?" he asks as he stands beside my table. The way he gazes at me is both sweet and commanding.

I nod, but don't say anything.

"What are you thinking?" he asks.

"I don't think your date is going to show up," I tell him.

"Clearly." His hand flings between us before he pinches the bridge of his nose. "I meant from earlier. My reading. What are you thinking?"

"Well, I'm … thinking … that … I …"

"I should have told you. I should have warned you."

"I think it was pretty clear you didn't know what book you were reading from today."

"Still, I should have told you about the book."

"It would have been nice to know."

"But you had to have some idea, right? After you read it."

Oye. I was hoping this part didn't come up.

I focus on the napkin under my water glass and even peel the corner off.

"You know, it's funny that you mention that, because I actually have not read that book."

"Really?"

"Or you know, any of your books."

"Are you being serious right now?"

"Yes."

His eyes go so narrow I have to lean forward a bit to make sure they are still open.

"You haven't read a single one of my books?"

I scrunch my face in answer.

"Wow."

He leans back in the booth and shakes his head.

"Who would have thought, right? Here I am thinking the worst of you all these years, and here you are pining over me like some lovesick puppy."

The noise that comes from him is indescribable, but he smiles for a brief moment.

"I'm not a lovesick puppy."

"Are you sure? Like I said, you did write a book about me."

"It was inspired by you, and that was the only scene I've ever written that actually happened to me."

"I see."

Silence stretches between us, and he rubs his palms to his eyes.

"So." I scratch my neck. "That was the night you got your first book deal, huh?"

He moves his hands to look up at me.

He nods.

"That's pretty cool," I say. Because it is. It would have been cooler if he had told me back then, but we can't change that now.

"Nora, I should have just gone to the table and told you about the phone call and asked you to come with me. We could have gone on our date after. Not showing up was—"

"A dick move," I finish for him.

"Yep."

Silence stretches between us.

"We should head back," I suggest.

He just nods.

We call an Uber, and like before, the ride back to the hotel is silent.

We hop in the elevator and—

"You know what," he says, startling me. He turns to face me. His right hand cups the side of my face, and I close my eyes as his thumb brushes my lower lip.

"What?" I barely hear the word myself.

"I'm sorry, Nora. You deserved better that night, and you probably deserve better now, but I just …"

"You just what?" I feel his body shifting closer to mine.

"I just can't seem to stay away from you."

He crashes his lips against mine and wraps his arms around my hips as I fall into his arms.

I didn't want to like this. I didn't want to like this one single bit, but my body doesn't care what my mind says. My hands race over his body, touching his chest, his arms, and then gripping his neck to deepen the kiss.

The ding when we reach our floor only speeds things up. We rush down the hall to my room. Hero tugs at my clothes—I tug at his. He nibbles on my lip—I nibble back. I want to give him everything he gives me. I want him to feel just as crazy as I feel. I want his heart to race like mine.

For as much as I didn't want this, I wanted it tenfold.

"Nora, how long have you wanted to do this?" he asks, sitting on the bed.

My mind freezes, but somehow, I still manage to breathe.

This is happening. It is really happening.

"I don't want to say."

"Tell me," he says and pulls my body snug to his.

Jesus, I wasn't sure we could get any closer, but he proved me wrong.

He hoists me up and over the bulge in his jeans, my legs on each side of his body as he leans back against the pillow, kissing my lips, my cheek, my jaw, my neck, and moving lower.

"Tell me," he says again.

"I … I … feel like I've wanted it forever. I wanted it back in college, and I've wanted it since you started showing up at my door at night."

He flips me over, keeping his body between my legs. His gaze is so intense that my breath hitches.

"You are absolutely amazing, Nora. You are smart, creative, funny, and beautiful. I've wanted to do this since college, too, and I swear I thought that I was over you, but then you moved to Wind Valley and came crashing back into my life. I don't …"

He trails off but never looks away from me. Whatever he's going to say next isn't going to hurt me. No, it's going to make me fall for him even more.

"I don't want to mess up this time. I want to do this right and take it slow and be all the things you deserve. I know I can give them to you if you'll give me the chance."

"What exactly are you asking?"

"Everything between us has been so sudden that I don't want you to have to make any rash choices at this moment, but I want to take you on a date. A real date. Not because I'm on some book tour promotion of dating women to find love, but because you want it and I want it."

Lord help me.

He kisses me again.

"I want it." I break the kiss for just those three words—then pull him back.

We start kissing like we'll never need air again. The only thing we need in the world is to be wrapped in each other's arms.

Even in my head I know it sounds corny, but god, it feels so right.

It feels right when his tongue tangles with mine.

It feels right when his hand slips under my shirt and his thumb brushes over my hard nipple.

It feels right when he grinds his hips into mine, his impressive erection exciting my body to a level I've never known before, and I can't seem to get his clothes off fast enough.

Everything feels right with Hero.

I should be scared of the unknown because we are about to make things very, *very* complicated, but I'm not.

I want him and he wants me—it's as simple as that.

I push him back slightly, enough room to lift my shirt over my head and toss it to the ground.

A small growl comes from the gorgeous man above me as he, too, whips his shirt off.

He dips his head to kiss me again, hard. Hard enough for me

to catch the hint that no matter how many more layers of clothing still need to be removed, we will not stop kissing.

He moves the kiss from my lips to my cheek to the jawline, then to my neck. Slowly, he presses his lips down my body. My hips lift to help him remove my pants. Then he reaches for the zipper of his jeans, standing at the side of the bed.

I'm lying here naked, ready to cross my arms in front of myself to hide, but he's smiling. The satisfied look on his face is all I need.

I move to my knees and help him wiggle down his jeans and boxers.

I let out a little whimper when his erection springs free.

God, how long has it been? I'm practically drooling at the sight.

"Lie back down, Nora," he says, and the demand in his voice gets me even more excited.

I do as I'm told. He grabs a condom from his pants pocket and sets it on the bed next to my head before crawling back over me.

His hands sneak under my backside, sliding down the bed until he reaches my butt. He lifts me quickly, moving me higher on the bed, and then shifts to put his head right between my legs.

"I love your butt. Did you know that?"

He grips it at the same time his tongue takes a long, slow stroke against my core.

"Oh god," I cry out and immediately run my hands through his hair.

"Yes, Nora, be vocal. I love it. Tell me when you like it and when you don't. Tell me when you want more and when you want me to stop. Tell me everything," he says, his lips brushing against my sex as he talks.

"That. Keep doing that, but harder."

This time his growl is loud and deep, and he does exactly as I tell him.

My entire body squirms in delight and my eyes close, the image of him between my legs filling the darkness.

He jerks me closer as the pressure builds and my release makes its presence known.

I cry out the moment he pulls back and shoves two fingers inside me.

"Oh fuck!"

"You're fucking beautiful, Nora." His eyes light up as I come down from my release and watch him roll the condom over his length.

"Wait, let me," I say and try to move, but he stops me with the shake of his head.

"Another night. Right now, after watching you come, I have to have you or I'm going to combust all over your bed and make a fool of myself."

His admission makes me smile.

"We wouldn't want that."

He chuckles. "No, we don't."

The smile fades instantly as he pushes me down onto my back. He places himself at my entrance.

"Do you want it slow and drawn out, or fast and hard?"

My chest heaves. I've never been with someone who asks me what I want, and Hero has made it clear that he wants me to enjoy every minute of this. He's putting me first, but I can see the fire in his eyes.

"Fast and hard." I kiss his lips and bite the lower one. "We have time to go slow later."

He presses into me hard, just like I asked. Oh, he feels so good. So amazing. I can hardly contain myself as I run my hands over my body and then over his shoulders and arms to hold on.

His hips pump on cue, and my body responds instantly. My legs wrap around him to hold him tight and my back bows, giving him better access to my breasts. He takes one in his mouth, sucking on it and letting it go with a loud pop.

"Shit, Nora. I'm not going to last long."

"Neither am I," I admit.

He stops and pulls out.

"I didn't mean—"

"Flip over," he instructs before I can finish my rejection.

I move fast. He grabs my hips to lift me and then enters me in another hard thrust.

"Holy shit!" I scream. Yes, this is perfect. So perfect.

His hips pound into me, and a feeling I know I won't be able to get enough of starts to creep slowly through my body, lighting me up. I push myself back into him to meet him thrust for thrust. He must sense that I'm about to get off because he reaches around to rub a finger against my clit. I come on contact, crying out in unison with his own groan.

We ride high until we both can catch our breath.

Hero disposes of the condom in the bathroom and comes back out to find me putting my pajamas on.

"What are you doing?" he asks, pausing naked in the doorway.

"Getting dressed?" I'm never sure what conversation to have after casual sex, and with Hero, the conversation will be even more complicated.

"Nuh-uh, naked and in bed, now. I'm staying over, and we are not even close to being done yet."

I press my lips to hide my smile, but it's impossible. He's right. What just happened is way better than talking. We can save that for another day.

I nod and crawl back into bed.

As soon as Hero joins me, he kisses me and snuggles in close.

This wasn't how I imagined my night ending. It's better.

CHAPTER TWENTY-FIVE

HERO

I need to get out of my last two dates.

I knew it the moment our lips touched at the bar the other night, and it wasn't even a question after last night. There is no way I should keep dating these women under false pretenses. No woman stands a chance against Nora. Not before, and especially not now.

I don't want to prove anything to anyone anymore to define my career. I just want to be with Nora.

But Doug spent an hour on the phone with me this morning, making some very good points on why I shouldn't stop this far in. The amount of people who are invested in this is insane, sales are better than ever, and two major streaming platforms have reached out to Doug with interest in my books. And it's official: I'm still in the running to win author of the year.

This survey is bringing my career to a level I never know it could reach. As much as I don't want to continue this, I don't see another way. Doug suggested I finish out the last two dates and then find a way to announce that I've met someone. I didn't tell him who, but I mentioned her name enough that I'm pretty sure he caught on.

I need to talk to her about it, but we both have places to be. Nora is meeting some of the other clients she represents who are signing here today, and I am meeting the guys for a quick last-minute writing session. It's the last stop we will all be at together.

I wanted to stay there in her room all day. I have all this lost time to make up for.

But fuck, I have a signing this afternoon and a date tonight.

"Is Simon coming today?" I ask the boys. The signing is in about an hour, but since it's nearing the end of the tour, our days are long, and coffee is very much needed in the afternoon. Being a single dad, Simon's tour gets changed up a lot so he can be home with his son, so I wouldn't be surprised if that was the case this time too.

I glance up at my friends, who are all head down into their laptops. One upside—or downfall—of a writing career is, you can do it anywhere at any time. Which means that even if you're supposed to be off on a vacation or taking a break, you don't.

"Bad Thai," Graham says. Just those two words.

"Is that a new book title?" I ask.

"No." He shakes his head. "Simon had bad Thai last night, so he isn't leaving his room for anything but the signing. He had Doug put him on the end of a row for any emergency exits."

Yikes. Been there, done that.

"Food poisoning is the worst," Zane chimes in without looking up.

"It really is and it …" Holy shit. That's it. I'm going to fake food poisoning tonight. It's brilliant. How did I not think of this before? Damn. I have some smart friends when I need them.

"Is what?" Grahams looks up.

I shake my head. What I intended to say is that it can ruin

anyone's night, but it’s probably best to not share how I plan to ruin a date later.

“Time!” Tobias shouts and shuts his laptop.

A collective set of groans fill our corner.

“Bad day?” I ask.

“For writing,” Zane says. “Did you write anything? Or was your plan to talk the entire time?”

“I didn’t talk the entire time, just at the end, and yes, I wrote words. Almost fifteen hundred in twenty minutes, thank you very much.”

Zane narrows his eyes at me, then nods. He knows that writing hasn’t been at the top of the list for me these days, so anything is better than nothing.

“A perky attitude. A great word count. Super chatty—oh. Oh!” he shouts and points at me. “Something happened with Nora, didn't it?”

His eyes go wide as he waits for my reply.

“With Nora?” Tobias chimes in. “Dude! What happened? Am I going to get yelled at? I told you to warn me. Actually, I told you to not do anything.”

I shake my head. “I don’t think you’ll get yelled at this time, trust me.”

“I’m not sure I believe it.”

“So, are you two like a thing now?” Beck asks. He was the only one who kept writing when Tobias called it. We give ourselves a timer, but we use it loosely. No one ever likes to end a session in the middle of a scene.

I shrug. “I’m not sure. Maybe? We haven't talked about it.”

“You should,” Tobias says solemnly.

“Is everything okay?” I ask him. “We might not be official, but I told her my intentions: I want to date her if she’ll let me.”

He nods. “I’m fine. It’s just that it’s Nora, man. I hate to be the one to say it, but you messed it up once before and Natalie didn't talk to me for a week. How long would she cut me off this time?"

"There won't be a *this* time. I'm not going to mess it up."

I'm a little annoyed at his accusation, but I can't blame him fully. He was a mess when Natalie wouldn't talk to him last time. This is years later, and the two are practically glued at the hip now. I don't think Natalie would ever do that again, but if I brought that up now, it would insinuate that I know her better than him.

"I swear," I assure him one more time.

"Don't fuck this up." He packs his bag, clearly ready to leave. "I need to do some shit before this thing later. See you guys there."

And just like that, Tobias is gone.

"I bet he's going to call Natalie," Zane says, watching our friend leave in a hurry.

"I haven't heard him swear like that in a while," Beck adds.

"Are you sure he and Natalie aren't dating in secret?" Graham asks.

"He is probably going to call her, I haven't heard anything either, and I think he would have told us. I didn't realize any mention of Nora and me would get him so wound up."

"You know what I think?" Zane says. "He's jealous. He's with Natalie almost every single day and they are just friends, and then here you come out of nowhere and win over a girl who has hated you for years. It's total jealousy."

Could that be it? We all think Tobias and Natalie are meant for each other, but there has to be a reason why they aren't together. Something the rest of us don't know. At the same time, Zane might not be totally wrong. Tobias doesn't really date. Is he waiting for Natalie to figure things out?

"You think that's all it is?" I ask.

"Dude, we all know he's in love with Natalie, and you just

did something that could jeopardize his time with her. What else could it be?"

Graham and Beck nod silently.

I'll have to talk to Tobias in a day or two when he has time to calm down. I didn't think my relationship with Nora would affect anyone else. I won't quit seeing her, but I will tell him that I don't mean any harm by it.

"We may as well call it for today," Graham says, following Tobias and packing up his stuff. We all end up doing the same, heading back to our rooms to freshen up.

As soon as this is over, I'm going to get a message to my date that I have food poisoning and then spend the night with Nora.

Easy peasy, lemon squeezy.

My date was at the signing. She saw me bright and cheery and laughing with others. She saw me and the guys heckle each other, and she saw me film a dancing reel with one of my readers. So, needless to say, I'm on my date tonight, and as soon as Nora took a quick video clip—yes video, not the average picture this time— she left without another word.

I feel like such a dick.

"So, then I was like, well, okay, I could totally sign up for this. I mean, what are the odds that he picks me?"

"I actually didn't pick any of the ladies I've gone out with. They were picked solely by which answers matched closest to mine on the survey."

"Oh, wow, so like, we are a match made in heaven. How close were our scores?"

"I'm not sure. My marketing manager handles all that."

"So you have no idea?" She leans back, crossing her arms over her chest and glaring at me. Her eyes narrow, and I swear I see flames shoot from her ears. That was a total 180 in personality.

"I do not."

"So what if we don't match on anything and we are not even compatible and this the biggest mistake of my life? This could be a total sham. Oh my god, what if we have nothing in common?" She follows a rather loud gasp by clasping a hand over her mouth.

I stare at her, thinking over my next words carefully.

"Nora wouldn't have selected you if we didn't match on at least four of the five questions."

"Oh my god," she shrieks. "I don't know why I didn't think of this before, but we totally only have four, maybe five things in common. That's not great. So, wings. Blue cheese or ranch?"

"I don't—"

"Blue cheese or ranch?" she screams at me.

"Blue cheese."

She blows out a breath. "Okay, that's good. Hardwood floors or carpet?"

I'm terrified to not answer.

"Hardwood floors."

She nods.

The next twenty minutes are similar, and if she isn't yelling at me to answer a random "this or that" question, her dramatics and loud voice have found another way to draw attention. If they didn't, then her declaration at the end of the date that she doesn't feel a spark should have done it. After all, I was still rising from my chair and grabbing my jacket when she started to walk away as she yelled it.

I can't say this was all my date's fault. I wasn't exactly in good spirits, but still, all I can think about is how fast an Uber can drive me back to the hotel and Nora.

Turns out, pretty fast if you have cash.

I hop into the elevator and press the number three. Unlike the hotels before tonight, Nora and I have an adjoining door. I was never a believer of fate, but if it was going to show up sometime in my life, it chose a pretty damn good day to do it.

I all but jog down the hall to my room, quickly changing out of my dress clothes and into something more comfortable. Then I knock on the adjoining room door.

Nora swings it open.

I rush in, my lips on hers before she can ask me why I'm back so early. I'm about two hours ahead of our nightly routine right now, but by the way her hands are clawing at my body, eager to remove every piece of clothing I have on, I'd say she isn't upset about this change of plans.

"I wasn't sure if you wanted to come over tonight," she says, swinging her shirt over her head.

She presses up on her toes to kiss me, and I take advantage of the moment by sneaking my hands around her and gripping her ass, lifting her to wrap her legs around me.

"I don't think I'm ever going to get enough of you."

"I sure hope not," she whispers into my ear before biting it.

Like a madman, I back us up to her bed and toss her onto it.

She lets out a giggle and then starts to shimmy out of her pajama pants. If there is any woman in this world who can make pajama pants sexy, it's Nora. The strappy tops she wears with them help. Especially when her nipples are poking through, but right now, she's already topless, and her breasts are perky and perfect as they call to me.

"What are you doing? Take your pants off," she says. Her bossy tone grows my erection immediately. Huh, who would have thought being bossed around would turn me on?

I unbutton and unzip my jeans, letting them fall to the ground as I stand over her.

"Tell me what you want me to do next."

With her next breath, her chest rises and her fingers tickle along her collarbone, stealing my attention. I want those to be my fingers touching her, but I want her to tell me to do it.

Her gaze narrows as she smiles. "You want me to make all the calls right now?"

"I do."

She moves her hand down her torso. "Do you think you can handle it?"

Fuck, I hope so.

"Yep."

Her eyes light up, and she puts her hands on her hips. "I really wish I had a whip right now."

I let out a deep chuckle and sit on the bed.

"Take all your clothes off." She points to my boxers. "Especially those."

It's very clear how turned on I am right now, and once it's evident to Nora, she yanks me onto the bed, climbing over my lap. With one leg on each side of me, she rubs against me.

"Oh lord," I breathe out. "Let me grab protection really quick."

"I'm on the pill. You know, if you want to … not."

Our eyes meet, and the passion and trust I see is all the confirmation I need that she means this.

I reach between us and position myself at her entrance. She lowers herself slowly, closing her eyes as I kiss her.

Nora Grayson.

I never thought I'd have her like this.

God, I'm a lucky, *lucky* man.

I should mention the idea of canceling my last date because it feels wrong to go out with someone else when I clearly know the woman I want is right here and waiting for me at the end of each night. But I'm not one to quit when I'm this close to the end of a task. Let alone one that has worked so well that my chances of winning author of the year could be even higher at this point.

I'll see this through.

Just one more date. After that, it's me and Nora. Together, officially. And we will find a way to announce it together. After all, the point of this is to find someone I fall in love with, and even if it didn't happen on a survey date, everything seems to be working out pretty well for me if I do say so myself.

CHAPTER TWENTY-SIX

NORA

These last couple of days with Hero have been nothing short of amazing. I can't believe I missed all this. Yet despite all the time we spent apart, it's like it never happened. God, this could have been us so long ago had we just talked. Had I given him the chance.

Now though, I'm giving him everything. I don't care that it's only been a few weeks since we have been back in each other's lives, this feels right.

I flip my card over, revealing a six. Hero does the same, only his is a ten.

"Dang it!" I close my eyes as if it's going to make me think better. "When I was eleven, I used to ride my bike to the corner of our street every day after school just to pet the dog that lived there. I would pretend he was mine and sit on the other side of the fence and talk to him."

Hero's bottom lip pops out, and he tilts his head. "That's adorable."

I shrug. "I was in between schools because we had just moved, so I didn't have a lot of friends."

His hand covers his heart. "That gives the story a whole new feel."

I shrug again. "Eventually, I got my own dog."

"Okay, let's flip. I can't hear any more about you substituting dogs for friends."

I giggle and he nudges me.

Then we flip cards again.

"Dang it. Why do I keep getting the small numbers?" I reach for his stack. "Did you rig this game?"

"I did not." He pulls his cards back out of my reach. "Take your turn."

This time, I tap my lips as I think.

Hero wanted a day for the two of us, so we opted for an afternoon of Door Dash with pizza and ice cream and games. Currently, we are playing one I made up. It's like war, but the person with the lowest card has to share something about themselves. It sounded fun before I started losing all the time.

"Oh! My mom once took me to this summer's eve event with witches, and for the whole next year, I swore I'd be a witch when I grew up."

Hero chuckles and starts to crawl toward me. "A witch, huh? Good or bad?"

"No way." I shove him back to a seated position. "We are playing this game."

We draw. I win.

"Yes! Finally!"

Hero chuckles again, this time leaning back against the headboard to get comfortable. A warm feeling sweeps over me, and I can't help but smile. Card games in bed was definitely a good idea. Especially since the last game left him in his boxers and me in nothing but one of his T-shirts.

"When my sister and I were kids, we had a pet lizard. It was the tiniest little thing, and we took care of him jointly. Well, it was my sister's weekend to watch him while I stayed with a friend, and when I got home, he was dead."

"Oh no."

He nods, his face expression serious.

"My sister was so proud to show me how well she did that as soon as I noticed he was dead, I said she did great and asked her to play outside with me. Then I asked my mom to distract her while my dad went to the pet store to get a new one. I replaced it before she found him."

"Aw, that's sweet."

"Yeah, it was sweet. Until the fifth time I did it and she asked me point blank how many I was going to buy before I just admitted that she shouldn't have an animal of any kind."

I let out a laugh, and he smiled.

"Are you close with your sister?"

"Yeah. We used to hang out all the time till she met her husband, and he moved her to New York."

"Aww." I rub my hand over his leg. "You miss her."

He nods. "I wish I saw my niece more, that's for sure. Are you close with your brother?"

I nod. "Yes."

"Is he enjoying his honeymoon?"

"I assume so. I talked to my mom yesterday and she said he sent her one text that said all is good. Flip?"

He doesn't even hesitate. He draws the smaller card again, and I smile.

"What else could I tell you? I've covered broken bones, tests I cheated on, failed driver's tests, classes I ditched, and now dead lizards."

"Such a wide variety."

"How about we change the rules on this one?"

I narrow my eyes as I study him.

"What did you have in mind?"

"I drew a three, so for three minutes, I can do anything to your body that I want."

I toss my cards down. "Hero Sebastian Quinn," I pause, enjoying that I now know his middle name. "You are relentless."

"Or just crazy about you. I'll let you decide."

He pushes the cards out of the way and moves closer to me.

I pretend to be annoyed as he handles my body as if I were weightless, tugging me against him and kissing my neck. One of his hands slips under the shirt I'm wearing, brushing me between my legs. I inhale.

A girl could get used to this.

Don't get me wrong, I'm having one of the best days of my life with Hero, but I get the feeling that neither of us are mentioning his last survey date on purpose. It's not like there is some grand prize for any of the women even if he does meet one he wants to see again, but after the last email conversation with the L-Mag, it's been suggested that Hero asks one woman from the tour to do an interview with him at the Lovers Magazine convention. It's completely different from winning author of the year, but of course Hero said he would consider it. Saying yes makes sense. Why wouldn't he? He'll do anything the L-Mag wants until author of the year is announced. He's worked too hard to lose it all now. I get that—as I've recently learned from the past and from the reading Hero did of his first book, his career will always come first.

So I'm not surprised he didn't cancel the last dates. A little bummed but not surprised.

I'd be lying if a little part of me isn't hoping he'll ask me to do the interview with him.

"When do the three minutes start?" I ask, ignoring my over-active mind and returning to a much more enjoyable moment.

"Right now."

He takes his time teasing me, building me up.

I eagerly grab my cards and shove them toward him when the time is up.

"Go."

We flip and this time, I get an ace over his four.

"Ace means I get as long as I want," I say. Then I smile and push him on his back.

I swear he growls. "Does it now?"

"Mm-hmm." I groan as his hand sneaks into my pajama shorts and begins rubbing over my panties. He tugs them to the side and slides a finger inside me.

Oh god. That's so much better.

"Spread your legs more," he says, then captures my mouth with his.

I comply and as soon as there is enough room, he shifts his body over me, adding a finger as he strokes me.

I bow my body on the bed, but he grabs my hips to steady me.

"Ah, ah, ah, don't try to crawl about if you want to be pleasured, Nora. You're going to feel every last bit of it."

He begins to pump his hand faster, and the whole idea that I had the winning card and should get to do what I want disappears. I'll do anything he wants as long as he doesn't stop.

"Oh god."

"Do you like that?"

"Yes."

"Good."

"I'm so close."

To torture me, he pulls his hand from between my legs.

"Hey," I shout, but I don't get another word in before his mouth is on me, replacing his hand, causing me to cry out. "Shit. Yes!"

His tongue flicks one, twice, and then his hand is back, and my body feels like it's out of control. My eyes are closed, but I don't need to see him to know what he's doing to me with every touch. My vision starts to blur, and my breath catches as a tingle zips through my entire body.

"Hero, yes! Oh yes, don't stop."

He works both his tongue and hand faster as I cry out, riding out my orgasm till the very last moment.

"Holy shit," I say when it's over and he looks up.

"Yeah?"

I nod and then drape an arm over my eyes as if it's going to help me catch my breath. "Yes."

"Good."

He lays down next to me, pulls me close, and kisses my shoulder. "What do you have planned for tomorrow?"

"Just work," I tell him.

"Anything specific?"

Doug and Hero's readers, if you go by the comments on his social media account, want an update on his search for love, and I have nothing to give them except that he is going on another date tonight.

"Just the norm," I tell him instead of mentioning the dates or the survey.

Here's your chance to ask him about it, Nora.

Take it.

Take it.

"Same." He kisses my temple once more. "I can't wait till the tour is over and we are back home."

My heart races, and I wrinkle my nose to tame the smile on my lips.

So what if he has another date with another woman? He basically just said he plans to be with me after the tour is over.

CHAPTER TWENTY-SEVEN

HERO

I'm on a date, and like the others, Nora is here—although not sitting with me—watching and taking notes for my online profile.

Just like the last one, I hate it.

I hate every minute of it.

I'm grumpy and anxious, and I feel like a total jerk.

Okay, so technically, I'm not on a date yet. Said date has yet to show up.

What are the chances that I get stood up twice?

My heart is pounding so loudly, I'm convinced the waiter can hear it each time he comes by the table.

I should just leave. I want to leave. But, fuck, I'm here for Nora. Ugh. Just everything feels wrong about this.

"Hi. Hero, right?"

I glance up to the woman hovering over the table and then stand quickly.

"Yes, that's me."

Okay, it's starting. I can do this.

"Oh, great." She beams a smile, but the slight twitch tells me she's nervous. "I've seen your picture. Obviously, right, since I've read your books, but everyone always looks so different in person."

"I agree. You must be Eloise."

"Yes."

"Please, have a seat."

She slides into the seat across from me and fidgets. Basically, her actions represent my thoughts.

"Is this weird?" Eloise asks.

"What exactly?"

"Dating all these random women on your tour, trying to find the one."

Trying. I already did, but that would be revealing more information than is needed right now. So I play along instead.

"Ah. Well, it's not exactly how I planned to meet someone, but weirder scenarios have happened to people." That's the truth. "Is this weird for you?" I ask.

Before she can answer, Nora steps up to the table. She looks gorgeous in just a simple pair of capri jeans with holes at the knees, a basic white T-shirt, and some flats. Her hair is pulled into a high bun, which I love because with her hair pulled back, I can see her eyes better. Nora has very telling eyes. I know when she's happy or mad, but right now, I really don't know what to make of what they are telling me.

She's avoiding my gaze, and I get it. It's the last date and neither of us wants me to be here.

We haven't said those exact words, but I know it's how we both feel.

"Can I grab a quick picture for the viewers?" she asks.

Eloise glances at me quickly, and I nod.

"This is Nora, she's my marketing manager."

And girlfriend in the making, I hope.

"Oh, of course."

Eloise and I both lean in and smile.

"Thank you," Nora says. "You two have fun. Don't forget about the terrace outside. Dinner out there would be lovely on a night like tonight."

And then she's gone.

I'm about to inch out of the booth to follow her, but my dates groans, distracting me.

She wrinkles her nose, laughs, and then covers her hands with her face.

"Gosh, I feel so guilty, but I can't sit here and lie."

Lie? Oh shit. What is she going to say?

"Okay…" I say, waiting for whatever she's about to reveal to me.

"I only entered this on a bet, and the only reason I said yes tonight was because I wanted to make my ex jealous. He thinks he's holding me back from a job, and so in his eyes that means we shouldn't be together. I thought if he saw me on a date ... well, he'd rethink things."

I nod slowly. I don't find this weird. It's relieving, having dinner with someone who isn't expecting too much from me. Since I have nothing to give. The pressure of the night instantly leaves my body on my next breath.

"How has it worked so far?" I ask, grabbing my phone to send Nora an "I'll see you soon" text. "Do you mind if I shoot a message off really quick?"

A light rosy color touches her cheeks.

"Not at all, and he called right before I walked in the door."

"Good." I grab the bottle of wine I'd ordered thinking I could take it back to the room if my date didn't show. Now that I know my date isn't expecting anything from me, I think we could both use a drink. "Do you want a glass? If it's working so far, you may as well get a free dinner out of it, right?"

Her shoulders visibly relax. "Really?"

"Really. I'm starving, and you set out on a mission. I'm not opposed to helping. I write romance for a living—I fully support falling in love."

Nora is going to love this when I tell her.

She laughs. "I suppose that's true. I'd love a glass."

"Great. Now, tell me about this job your boyfriend thinks he's holding you back from."

As much as I'd love to end this date right now and head back to Nora, finishing this date is the right thing to do. This woman has set out to win a man back—who am I stop her when I plan to win over a woman of my own?

"I'm a teacher, and I've been teaching in Europe for the last few years."

"That's awesome."

"It's a little crazy. I teach at a private school for some very elite families. You wouldn't believe the number of students who have bodyguards escort them to my classroom."

I lean forward to hear more. I'm not just putting up an act either. This sounds like something that would fit for a new book.

"Do you mind if I ask you more questions about this? I'd love to take notes and add it into a book."

"You haven't even heard my story yet." She sips her wine.

"No, but I can already tell it's going to be a good one."

Eloise and I spend the remainder of the night sipping wine, snacking on artichoke dip, and eating dinner. Her story is one I want to hear more of, so I get her contact information as I walk her to her car.

I enjoyed myself, and Eloise's background is interesting, but this moment right here, the one where I say goodnight to my date and return to the hotel and go straight to Nora, is the part I look forward to most.

CHAPTER TWENTY-EIGHT

NORA

The rain is pelting against my hotel window so hard that I can barely think. I woke up early this morning to get a little extra work done before Hero woke up.

I glance over at the bed. I can't believe he's sleeping through this. It woke me up on and off all night.

I try to refocus on the laptop in front of me. Typically, I stay up late into the night to get work done, but for obvious reasons that are still in my bed, that did not happen. I need to get something done.

A loud siren noise fills the room, coming from both my cell phone and Hero's. I read the notice that our flight back to Wind Valley, since the tour and Hero's dates are over as of yesterday, has been delayed due to weather just before a movement catches my attention. He sits up quickly. He doesn't go for his phone right away, but I can see the panic in his eyes when he discovers I'm not next to him.

"Good morning. Our flight is delayed until the afternoon."

He gives me a playful look, grabs his phone, and stalks over to me. He sits next to me, grabs my chair to slide it closer to him, and then grabs my hips to put me on his lap. With one leg on each side of him, I settle in and press my lips to his.

It's a soft and sweet kiss. Perfect for the morning.

"How about you don't scare me like that anymore," he says, resting his forehead against mine.

"I was three feet away," I say with a laugh.

"Yeah, but I'm growing accustomed to waking up with you next to me. Not with you sitting at the table in our room watching me."

"My bad." I give him one more kiss.

I intended for this one to be just as sweet and simple as the last, but Hero clearly has other plans. His tongue invades my mouth. I'm in one of his shirts and my underwear only. I can feel everything as he grows beneath me, and my desperate body clings to his for more.

One of his hands moves to the back of my head, curling into my hair to kiss me harder. His other hand squeezes between our bodies until he reaches his destination between my legs.

"Oh," I say on a breath.

"This is why you should be in bed with me. I can't seem to get enough of you. How long is the flight delayed?"

"Four and a half hours," I barely breathe out.

"Perfect."

He moves my underwear to the side and begins rubbing his fingers against my bare skin. My hips have a mind of their own as they rotate with him.

"You're so responsive to me, it drives me crazy."

You know what drives me crazy? The way he speaks to me when we are in positions like this. He speaks as if I'm the only thing that matters and like I'm the only thing he wants. What kind of a woman wouldn't have a reaction to that?

"Let's move to the bed," I say, grabbing his face and kissing him.

Our lips are still connected as he shakes his head. "Not yet."

He pulls his hand away from me, and I let out a small whimper, only for it to quickly turn into a gasp when he grabs me by the hips, sets me on the table, and spreads my legs right in front of him. "Every time I see you working at this table, I get this image of me doing this to you on it. Even that first night after I showed up at your room, I knew I had to have you."

"That was a different table," I say as he licks my inner thigh, working his way toward my panties.

"It's not the table that gets me this worked up, Nora."

Hooking a thumb at each side of my waist, he pulls my panties off, leaving me bare in front of him.

Just when I think he's about to say something about the view, he surprises me again by eagerly leaning forward and placing one slow lick of his tongue against me.

My butt bucks off the table; he drapes an arm over me to hold me down.

"I'll make it quick if that's what you want."

"Please, yes."

I run a hand through his hair as he goes down on me right on the hotel table with a bright screen displaying my open document in Excel next to me.

Damn. I'll never look at spreadsheets the same way again.

I close my eyes, living in this moment with Hero. God, all those years. All those years. If I had just heard him out back then, I could have been having this my entire life.

"Ah!" I cry out as my release builds inside me. My legs twitch, and my knees clap against his head, but that doesn't stop him. He only increases his pace and as soon as I tell him I'm coming, he replaces his tongue with two fingers, sending a whole new wave through me. My hips lift from the table, riding his fingers until my release ends.

Holy shit.

I have no words for what this man just did to me.

Through a growl, I'm whisked off the table as if I weigh nothing. Hero moves to the bed, lays me on it, and my body instantly calls out to him. I lock a heel around his waist to pull him onto me.

"You're taking too long," I tell him, flipping him over and climbing over him.

"By all means," he says. "Punish me."

And I do. Two more times before we order room service for breakfast and before I see the email from the L-Mag. The email that informs Hero that they are so impressed with his response to their review that instead of just an interview, they'd love to host a dinner and date night for Hero and the lady of his choice from the dates at the Lovers Convention. All expenses paid for both of them, and they'd love to do the interview at that time. All he has to do it let them know who he's chosen.

It's not a new request from them, and even though I'm thrilled the dates are over, it still remains that Hero has yet to ask me to do the interview with him.

If he's going to.

He is.

He will.

Right?

CHAPTER TWENTY-NINE

HERO

It feels amazing to be home. To be done with the tour, the dates, to be back to a life I love and with a wonderful addition to it. Nora. My family is going to be thrilled.

I step into my parents' house and hear the baby giggles immediately. I saw the car outside, so I had a feeling my sister was in town, but since she flies in from New York and has a rental every time she visits, you just never know.

"Hello?" I call out as I step farther into the house.

"Oh my god, he's here!" My sister's excited voice fills the room. "I wasn't sure you'd make it tonight."

"It's Sunday, Sydney," I tell her. "Mom cooks every Sunday, and if I can make it, I always do."

"Yeah, well, we thought that maybe with the new love of your life, you might be busy."

My dad tries to hide his smile with his hand, but my mom and sister are already full of smiles.

"Love of my life?" I ask.

Who would have told them about Nora and then referred to her as that? Not that I disagree.

"Wasn't that the point of the tour?" Sydney says, bringing me back to the conversation. "Did you meet anyone on your dates that we should be expecting an introduction to?" She's on fire with questions tonight. In fact, she's been a little too invested in my love life since she and her husband worked things out for themselves.

I sit and sigh, which in my sister's eyes is a reason to cheer.

"Who is she? Tell us all about her."

"For starters, I didn't meet her on any of the dates."

"Huh?" Dad says.

"Even better. Go on," Sydney says.

I reach down to grab my niece, who is having floor time on a Paw Patrol busy mat and put her in my lap.

"It's Nora, my marketing manager."

"Oh my god, *the* Nora?"

"What do you mean, *the* Nora?" I ask with my best impersonation of her tone.

She shrugs. "Zane mentioned her once. I thought she hated you."

I jerk my head back but keep a smile on the tiny face in front of me.

"How much did Zane tell you?"

"Enough for me to know that you are most definitely leaving details out."

Oh, I have details, but they aren't for my sister's or parents' ears.

"Ohhhhh," Sydney laughs. "I get it now. You can tell me later."

"How about we just eat?" I suggest as I hear the oven timer go off.

"He's in a rush, Mom," Sydney teases. "He must be going to see Nora after this."

"Stop teasing your brother," Mom says as she passes Sydney to the kitchen.

Dad follows her, and I nudge Sydney's foot with mine as I keep hold of my niece. "Yeah, don't tease me."

"No problem. I'll leave that for Nora."

My eyes go wide, and I glance toward the kitchen. Thankfully, my parents didn't hear that. Because let's face it, she's not wrong. Nora knows exactly how to tease me, and I plan to enjoy a little bit of it when I leave here.

I take my seat at the table.

I'm about to set a record on how fast I can eat.

I texted Nora as soon as I left my parents' house to tell her that I was headed over, and she told me to let myself in when I got here.

She's sitting in one of the spare rooms that's slowly becoming her and Natalie's office.

"I thought we could go grab some ice cream and settle in with a movie tonight."

Her reply is instant. "I'm busy, maybe another night."

"I could grab everything and bring it back here. I'll pick up my computer, too, and we can make it a working date night."

"Maybe another night. Really, Hero, I'm swamped here."

She hasn't looked up once since I stepped into her office, and her tone reminds me of those first few days we spent together. The days before the tour even started. I rise from where I am sitting in Natalie's workspace chair.

Still, she doesn't even look in my direction.

I'd ask her again if things are okay, but she's told me twice now that she's working, so she's not going to dive into any kind of conversation right now.

My heart clenches. I don't want to leave. I just spent every day for the last two weeks with her. I want to hang out with her. Leaving feels wrong.

I knock my knuckles against her door.

"I'll text you later then?"

"Sure."

Sure.

That's almost as bad as *fine*.

I step toward her desk to kiss her goodbye, but her phone rings.

"Nora Grayson," she answers and then covers the mouthpiece to look at me. "We'll talk later, okay?"

I nod and duck out so she can get back to work.

I'm sure I'm just overthinking it. We're still trying to figure out this whole real life and dating vibe we have going. She's a workaholic, and I like to work too. Maybe next time I'll bring my computer, and then when she wants to sit quietly to get some things done, I'll do the same. Doug has been hounding me about my next book anyway. I should probably buckle down and finish it.

As soon as I get in my car, I glance at Nora's front window. I can see her walking through her house, arms waving as she talks on the phone.

I smile. I always wondered if I would ever find the one that I wanted more than I wanted to write. It's a relief.

There was a time in my life where I thought this moment wouldn't come for me. I'm only thirty, but still, outside of my group of friends, almost everyone I know is married and has kids.

I back out of her driveway and head for my place, thoughts of Nora on my mind.

I hope this phase of learning how to navigate real life together doesn't last long.

I miss her already.

But as soon as I get home, an email comes through.

It's from Eloise, the mafia schoolteacher. She's passing through Wind Valley and would love to get coffee tomorrow if I have time.

I glance at the clock, then at my word count.

At this point, I'll do anything to pass the time until Nora reaches out.

I spend the rest of the night replying to emails. Well, all except one. I'd planned to talk to Nora tonight about how she thinks we should reply to this L-Mag request. My thoughts are to tell them exactly what happened, that Nora will be the one to accompany me on the interview. I just want to go with the honest truth. I never considered us as hiding while on tour, but as soon as Nora said it, I knew that's how she felt.

I never want her to feel that way again, and as soon as I see her, I'm going to kiss her and hold her and make sure she knows that's she's it for me.

CHAPTER THIRTY

NORA

Work has been crazy in the last couple of days since we've been home from the tour. Especially when it comes to the follow-up on the survey dates for Hero. Followers want to see the happily ever after, so I'm not surprised at the remark my cousin just made to me.

"We have to give them something. Some of his readers are tweeting that it was all an elaborate stunt to help his books sales. We can't let this backfire on us," Doug argues.

I rub my temples and close my eyes. "Why are people so invested?"

"Because it's Hero Quinn, Nora. One of the few male romance writers out there who write strong, confident women as their heroines and somehow still manage to make everyone fall in love with a controlling, angry hero. But one wrong move for him at this stage in his career could break him."

"I think you're being a tad bit dramatic."

"This is your job, Nora. What's our next move?"

"Let me think about it."

"Think fast, because if I make one more phone call and neither of you have an answer for me, I'm going to lose my shit."

"Okay, I'll come up with something."

That something would be talking to Hero about who he's taking to the Lovers Convention. His choice will be a great feature to feed his followers, but I don't know the answer. He hasn't replied to their email yet, or if he did, he didn't include me on the response.

"Thank you, and if he isn't bringing anyone to the convention, we can use that too."

Did he say that to Doug?

"Oh, he isn't bringing anyone?" I ask, praying my voice is calm and cool.

"Not from his dates," Doug says in a knowing tone. "But he might bring someone else … like you."

I laugh out loud.

"Don't laugh at me, Nora. You know I'm right."

Is that what Hero told him when they talked?

"Who told you that he'd bring me?"

"I figured it out on my own."

I laugh again. "Doesn't mean you're right."

He sighs, loudly. "Just get me an answer by the end of the day. Goodbye, Nora."

"Good—"

Okay, call over.

Finding Hero and clearing things up is the smartest choice. Then my mind can stop wondering about all the what ifs.

Plus, if my cousin is right and Hero is planning to bring me, I want to know. I've pushed him away since we've been home because I've been worried that he won't pick me. But clearly, Doug knows something, right? He wouldn't say that if Hero didn't mention it.

"What are you thinking about?" Natalie asks as she comes into our office and sits across from me.

"Nothing." I sigh.

"The ole dramatic sigh is definitely nothing."

"Hero's readers need a follow-up on his dates. If I don't produce something, it will seem as though it was all a marketing stunt. I don't know what to do."

I know what I want to do, but again, I need to go talk to Hero.

"Um, post your face and his face and call it fate."

I roll my eyes.

"We … haven't exactly talked about us."

"And whose fault is that? Tobias mentioned that you've been avoiding Hero."

"I'm not … he said that?"

She nods. "Well, he said that Hero told him you've been a little different since we got home, that making time hasn't been at the top of your list, and he is trying to respect your work ethics. But I know you, and you're avoiding him."

I groan.

"It all just happened so fast. What happens when … when he changes his mind? Or what if I'm sitting at a table in a restaurant waiting for him again and something with work pops up and he never makes it?"

I know it's a stretch, but it's very clear that his career is important to him. Add in the fact we haven't defined who we are and that this whole thing is bigger than we imagined, I just want us to make the right choice. For everyone.

Natalie gives me a soft smile and then joins me, sitting on the armrest. "I don't think he's going to change his mind."

"He did it before."

"That was years ago. He's not the same guy anymore. Plus, it wasn't like he changed his mind over you specifically. You told me it was because he had an opportunity with his career that he couldn't pass up on."

"Exactly. What if he gets another one and leaves me in the dust again? I'm not sure I can open up my heart just to get burned again."

"Again, I don't think that will happen, but avoiding him won't do either of you any favors. The two of you also need to figure out how you want to solve the survey thing. You're a team now, in more ways than one. Go find him."

I nod. "You're right. I'm just … ugh, I'm scared."

"That's how you know it's right. Go talk to him now. I still have a few things to do before I call it a day."

I stand up, grabbing my phone to call him. He doesn't answer.

I don't want to dwell on all of this, so I pull up one of the social media apps that lets you see the location of others. He's at the coffee shop.

Oh, he's probably writing.

And he didn't answer your call.

No. No. That doesn't mean he would pick his work over me again. It just means he's working. I don't answer my phone sometimes when I'm working either. It's nothing personal.

"He's at the coffee shop. Lock up when you leave," I say to Natalie as I move through the kitchen and grab my purse off the back of my chair.

I rush to my car.

Ugh. We've been home for a few days now, and I've been ruining what could be great just because I'm scared. I can't do that. I really like Hero. Despite everything that happened, it's clear he isn't the same guy he used to be. It's not fair for me to compare him to anyone but the man he is today.

The drive to the coffee shop is quick. I practically sprint from my car to the front door, only to pause in front of the big window.

Hero is sitting with a woman. They are both laughing, and he is leaning forward to look at something on the table. Whatever it is makes him laugh even harder.

This woman looks familiar.

Very familiar.

Was she … no, it's not possible. None of his dates live in Wyoming. If she was one of them, she made a special trip here. Which means … what? That he fooled me? That he'd rather save his career by picking one of the dates than by picking me?

I grab my phone and pull up his social media feed. He said the last date intrigued him the most. Immediately, her face pops up in the photo I took of them. It's the same face of the woman sitting across from Hero.

What is happening?

I move my hand to the door handle, ready to go in there and ask him, but can't force myself to do it.

This is exactly why I didn't want to get my hopes up. His job means everything to him and so does his reputation. He picked one of the dates because that's what his readers and the L-Mag want. That's what he needs to win author of the year.

He chose his career over me again.

It's as simple as that, and yet my heart still hurts more than I could have ever imagined.

CHAPTER THIRTY-ONE

HERO

It's Wednesday. We are writing or supposed to be writing. I can feel everyone staring at me, but I'm on a roll with this book and don't really want to stop to talk.

"Time," Tobias says, and a string of *thank god* and *finally* float around the room.

I glance around the group, and sure enough, they are all looking at me.

"What?"

"What do you mean *what*?" Tobias speaks up first. "What the hell happened?"

I blink and then point at my computer. "I was writing. You know, the whole reason we meet up. It's totally crazy, but one of the dates Nora set me up with has a badass backstory of working with kids of mafia families, and I twisted it into my new story. I even met with her yesterday when she and her boyfriend were passing through town and—what? Why are you all looking at me like I said I just found a dead body?"

"She was a date?" Zane asks.

"Who?"

"The woman at the coffee shop. Shit, Hero, keep up," Tobias says, clearly frustrated.

"Keep up." I toss my hands up. "You guys are the ones acting weird."

"So you didn't end things with Nora?"

"No, and who the hell told you that?" I cross my arms.

They all look at Tobias.

His eyes go wide. "Natalie said he did, and given his history, I believed her."

"You better tell me what the hell is going on right now." I lean forward. Moving my computer out of the way, I rest my forearms on the table and pin Tobias with a glare. "And tell me everything. Including what you swore to Natalie that you wouldn't tell me."

"I can't—"

"Tobias!"

He cringes.

"Nora saw you with this woman at the coffee shop. She was already feeling uneasy, thinking you'd pick work over her again, and then Doug called her and said she had to post a follow-up to the survey thing. She didn't know what to do, because the two of you hadn't exactly defined your relationship. So she went to talk to you and saw you with this woman. She figured out it was one of your dates. In her eyes, you picked your career again. You picked one of the dates to announce online instead of her to save your image. She told Natalie it was over."

Fucking hell. This is why she's been avoiding me? I should have known it wasn't just that she was busy with work.

Fuck.

Things between us are still new, and I didn't know her normal work schedule and fuck, I should have known.

I can't believe I didn't put this together first.

I can't lose her. Not when I just got her.

Instead of explaining myself to my friends, I ditch my laptop and everything else I'd brought with me and grab my keys off the kitchen island as I head out the door.

We are not over. We're not. It's a misunderstanding, and I'm not going another seven years without her just because we can't communicate.

I hit my hand against the wheel as I drive. "Damn it!"

I knew something was up this entire week. We didn't talk at all yesterday. I thought maybe she needed space. I wanted her to see that I respected her time alone. I didn't want to overwhelm her.

Fuck. I should've just gone with my gut and gone to her. I've fucking missed her since we have been back, and now she thinks we are over. Fuck.

I pull up in her driveway, noticing Natalie's car there as well.

I get out, run to the door, and start knocking. I want to pound on it and rush in without waiting, but I remain as calm as I can.

Natalie opens the door.

Her eyes go wide. "Hero, what are you doing here?"

"I need to talk to Nora."

Natalie steps back to let me in, and I find Nora sitting at the kitchen table with her arms crossed.

"Why are you here?"

"To talk about the coffee shop and the fact that we are indeed *not* over."

Nora's face remains expressionless for a slight moment before one brow rises and she glares at her best friend behind me. "How much did you tell Tobias?"

Natalie makes a *yikes*! face and shrugs. She looks down in defeat as she says, "Pretty much all of it."

"Natalie!"

"I wanted to find out what happened, but Tobias didn't know anything. He said we probably saw it wrong because Hero is one of the best people he knows. Clearly," she points at me, "Tobias was onto something."

It's nice to know that even though he can't be straight with me and tell me how it is in person, he'll defend me when I'm not around.

Good friends are hard to find, and I've got the best. At the same time, a great partner is also hard to find, so I'm not leaving till we fix this.

"I'll just go," Natalie says and grabs her purse, walking out the front door.

I move to the seat closest to Nora.

I'm about to dive right in, but she speaks first.

"We need to post a follow-up to your dates. I was thinking we could do a reveal on your pick. Something slow, though, a tease if you will, for your readers. I've drafted a few posts." She spins her computer so that I can see the screen.

"I'm not here to talk about work."

"Well, we don't exactly have a relationship outside of it, so—"

"We do." I lean back, crossing my arms as I watch her.

Her lips part as she takes a breath, and her eyes flash to meet mine. As soon as her tongue sweeps over her lips, I reach for her chair and scoot it closer to me. Her knees knock against mine as I cup the back of her head and pull her in for a kiss.

Her fingers clench my shirt as I deepen the kiss.

This right here, this passion and heat and desire we have for each other, is why this isn't over. Even if we aren't seeing eye to eye, you can't keep us apart.

I slide my hands to her hips, tugging just enough that she gets the hint to move from her chair to mine. She does, straddling me over the chair and wrapping her arms around me. Our lips never part as our bodies melt together.

"I've missed you," I say, breaking the kiss.

But that's all the time she needs to bolt off me.

"We shouldn't have done that."

She backs up until she bumps into her kitchen island.

"Nora, look, nothing is going on with the woman from the coffee shop. I met with her to take notes on a book and —"

"This isn't going to work."

"What?"

I don't think I heard her right.

"Things between us need to stay professional only. Can we leave it at that?"

"No, we can't leave it at that."

"That's all you get."

"Tell me what you're thinking."

"No. You should probably go."

"I'm not leaving."

"Please, Hero."

My heart and mind argue with each other, but my heart wins. "I'm not leaving till we figure this out."

She sighs, like she always does when she's annoyed.

"I just want to understand what happened. Why didn't you come to me when you saw me with someone else?"

She shrugs. "It just made sense to me."

"It made sense that I would spend time with you, and then go find another woman?"

"That when it comes to your career, you'll pick it over me every time."

"I'm a little lost."

"The L-Mag, Doug, your readers … they wanted a follow-up to the survey. It looks better if you pick one of your dates. So you did. Career saved, books back on the best sellers, author of the year secured, and Nora … left behind."

"That's not what happened, Nora. I—"

"You should leave."

"I don't want to leave until we figure this out. You're not even giving me a chance to—"

"There is nothing to figure out, Hero. If you ever have to pick between me or your career, it will always be your career. I'm not enough for you, and I get it now."

"Not enough for me?" I grab her hands and pull her close. "Not enough for me, Nora? You're everything to me."

"Then why haven't you asked me to go with you to the L-Mag conference? Not as your marketing manager, but as the woman you chose. The woman to do the interview with?"

"I was go—"

Both our phones ping at the same time, followed by her computer. She sighs and sits to look at the screen.

I couldn't care less about what message just came through. I want to fix this.

"Look, Nora, you are—"

"You're officially author of the year," she says, cutting me off and turning her computer to face me. "Congratulations."

The lack of excitement in her voice matches exactly how I feel.

I shake my head, ignoring the news that I thought would make my entire life, and stare at the woman in front of me. I kneel to grab her hands, but she stands and storms off toward the living room. I figure she's going to take a seat on the couch, but she keeps moving until she opens the door and points for me to go.

Fuck. This was not how this was supposed to go.

"Please go."

I don't want to. I want to stay and fight, but if I stay, it could chance one of us saying something we can't take back.

"Fine, Nora. If you want me to leave, I'll leave. Not because I'm giving up, but because I want you to get what you want in this life. If that's me leaving, then so be it. But I wasn't meeting her because I chose her over you. I was meeting her for research on a book. That's all. If I pick anyone, it's you."

I head for her door, where I stop and turn.

"For the record," I start, waiting for her to look up. She doesn't. "This thing between us isn't over yet. I'll admit we rushed things, but I don't care. I want to be with you. If you feel even the slightest way about me, don't give up on us, okay?"

I wait for a reaction of any kind, but I get none.

My phone starts to go off in my pocket on the drive home, but even once I'm in my kitchen, I don't look.

What's there to celebrate?

I just lost the person I want more for the *thing* I used to want most.

How the hell do I fix this?

CHAPTER THIRTY-TWO

NORA

"Is it absolutely necessary that I come?"

I curl my legs into my body as I sit on the couch in my living room. I've been thinking of a way to get out of the *Lovers Magazine* convention all week. It's the big one. The end-of-summer book bang of all reader book signings and writer workshops. Hundreds of authors and thousands of readers. It's an event no one wants to miss. Unless you're me.

I can't see Hero. Not yet. We live in the same town and hang out with the same people. It's inevitable that we will see the other, but if I can delay it, I will.

I let myself fall too hard and too fast for him, only to have my heart broken all over again.

I'm not ready.

Hero and I went from never speaking to waking up in the other's arms in a matter of weeks. I just wish … gosh, I don't even know what I wish anymore.

A long sigh fills the other end of the phone line.

"Look, Nora, I guess you don't have to be there. I just thought that with the guys moving forward with this joint series they want to write and with you being the marketing manager for all of them, this would be a great opportunity to get together. I'd like you to be there, but since you all live in the same town, I suppose if you all meet up and want to Zoom call me in one afternoon, that's fine as well."

So Doug is telling me that, either way, I will have to come face-to-face with Hero.

"I'll come to the conference," I give in. It's the coward's way out. At least there, I can make up an excuse to leave for work—here in Wind Valley, he could follow me out the door or to my house. Technically, he can do all those things at the conference, but he'll also want to be professional, and the last thing he will want to do is cause a scene.

"That's really great, Nora. That's the right choice. If you're that worried about seeing Hero, don't forget that I have to send you the conference schedule for all my clients attending. What you do with the information on Hero's whereabouts is up to you."

At least there is that, but still, I am amazing at what I do, and this is my job. I can suck it up for one week. Being anything but professional at this conference would be doing just that, so I'm going, and I'm going to be a big girl. Even if I end up in my room crying all night long.

"Thanks, Doug."

"Now, as your cousin—dude, how are you going to manage this? He's author of the year at this thing. His face will be everywhere, and people will be talking about him nonstop. Are you going to avoid him?"

I can't help but smile. Doug would go all dramatic on me after a serious conversation.

"I'm not sure yet."

"You do know he isn't bringing anyone, right? He told the L-Mag that it didn't work out with any of the blind dates."

I figured as much since the L-Mag hadn't advertised that Hero would be with his date, and because Natalie has been working his account for me, well, I know she would have told me by now if he had chosen someone. She knows being caught off guard would hurt more.

"I sensed that, yeah."

"I don't have lunch plans with any of the guys the entire week I'm there. I planned it as little break from work, which also seems like a great time to have some one-on-one time with my favorite cousin."

"I don't want to take up the only time in your schedule for yourself, Doug."

"I'll be more insulted if you don't join me—and Nora, he's miserable without you too. I'm not sure what happened in those weeks you two had together, but it meant something to him."

I hold the phone away from my face to sniffle and then I take a breath.

"See you at the conference, Doug."

"Night, Nora."

CHAPTER THIRTY-THREE

HERO

I've never been so nervous in my life, and that says a lot.

"Are you sure she's going to be here?" I ask quietly, leaning over to Zane. He's sitting next to me on the current panel. After this, we have about ten minutes before the evening awards ceremony. I know I'm receiving an award. The biggest award for our industry, but I'm still meh about it.

I'm glad readers are happy, but if there is anyone that I want to please most in this world, it's Nora. I sure as hell hope she's here today so I can make that happen. Making the grand gesture while I'm up on stage has set my nerves on edge, but she's worth it.

We are dismissed from the panel, and the two of us make a beeline out of the room. I can't be late. Everything is riding on this.

"Yeah, Tobias even said he saw her with Doug at breakfast this morning. She bailed as soon as she saw him, though. He considered going after her, but considering your plans, he chose not to spook her into not leaving her room for the rest of today."

"Well, that's better than nothing, I guess."

"You're sure about this?" he asks.

I nod.

"I meant what I said to her. This isn't over for me. She's my everything. She's the only one I want to share my life with."

He lets out a breath.

"Then I'm not even going to ask what happens if she turns you down, because that clearly isn't an option."

I keep my eyes on the lookout as I make my way to the conference room. This can go one of two ways: it will work out or it won't work out, and I'll have the rest of the week to avoid seeing her.

Or I'll make more and more attempts to win her back. That's a much better plan.

I'm leaving this conference with her on my arm. That is my goal. It's the only goal when you're in love.

Doug waves at me as I walk into the room. I scan the room for any sign of Nora.

She's not here.

Yet.

* * *

"Do you have your next book planned out? Is there a next book? What's next for your readers?"

My eyes search the crowd as the L-Mag interviewer, Mina, rattles off question after question. Still no sign of Nora.

After I told the L-Mag that I didn't click with any of my dates, I expected some sort of pushback. Especially since they just named me author of year. Although, I guess I should have known they'd respond kindly since they announced me as winner, even before I replied with the news of not picking a date. I didn't mention Nora, though. With the way she and I left things, I didn't want to say anything that could backfire on me later with her.

Which is why I'm glad they haven't asked about the surveys yet. Maybe I'll get lucky, and they won't ask questions.

Suddenly, the back door opens and Nora walks in. Our gazes lock immediately.

Instantly, I can see that she wants to flee, so if this is my only chance, even if it wasn't my original plan to win her back, I'm going to take it while I have it.

"Well, Mina, I'm glad you asked. I've got a love story in the works, but the heroine is a bit more stubborn than I'm used to."

"Can't you just rewrite her?"

"Not this one," I say and shoot Nora a wink. "I don't want to change her. I want to write this story with her. I just need her to want it too."

"You keep saying *her*. As if you know this woman personally, so that brings me to the question everyone is dying to know: did you find love on tour? I was informed that sadly, you did not, but I'm getting a different vibe from you right now."

Eyes still locked with Nora's; I nod.

"I actually did, yes. Very much."

The room erupts into a mix of noises. People are thrilled with my answer.

"Tell us more."

"What do you want to know?"

"Does she feel the same?"

"I sure as hell hope so."

"When do we get to meet her? Or at least hear her name?"

"I'm not sure about that one because, you see, I may have already messed it up before it even had a chance to start."

A collective gasp fills the room.

"Oh, wow. Can you explain that?"

"Not really. Love isn't something that can be forced, and

while I think I fell in love with this woman years ago, the choices I made when I was younger have hindered my chances now."

"So, this is an old flame?"

I shake my head. "No. She was a woman I'd invited to dinner one night and then I never showed."

The room is silent and the interviewer's eyes are wide. "Wow. I wasn't expecting that."

"I wasn't expecting her."

"So, what now?" Mina asks and then she laughs. "We are getting off subject and prying too much into your life, Hero. I'm sorry."

"It's fine. She's actually in this room right now."

Like before, a rustle of noise takes over as people shift in their seats to look around and whisper to each other.

"So what now?" I echo. "I'm in love with her. I've always been in love with her. And I will wait for her. As long as it takes."

And it's the honest truth.

CHAPTER THIRTY-FOUR

NORA

Holy shit.

The room is buzzing as everyone looks around. No one has spotted me, but I still lean forward and back as if I'm searching for this mystery woman too.

Back and forth, back and forth. Side to side. Anything that lets me avoid eye contact with Hero.

If anyone paused to look at me longer than a few seconds, they would see the sheen of sweat on my forehead or the way I can't stop fidgeting.

He loves me.

Hero Quinn is in love with me.

Holy shit.

The award is the only reason I'm here. I wanted to snag a couple pictures of him receiving it for his page.

After the room quiets down, the interviewer who is also going to be giving Hero his award here in a few minutes, continues with questions.

An interview where he tells everyone he loves me was not what I was expecting.

It's been only a couple weeks since I held the door open for Hero to leave my house, but he hasn't reached out once. As soon as he explained himself and told me he was just meeting with her about a book, I knew I'd messed up. I mean, I blatantly told him that I didn't trust him.

"So tell us, Hero, why didn't you show up to dinner? If this woman means that much to you, why stand her up? Why should she trust you now?"

"Because he's not the same person he was before, Mina, and until this very moment, I don't think I fully understood that." I turn quickly, rushing out the door to the large convention hall and speed walk for the elevators.

I can't listen to him tell that entire room how he loves me, knowing how I treated him. I have to come up with a way to show him that I'm sorry and that I love him too.

"Nora, wait!"

I spin around quickly.

"What are you doing?" I ask in panic. "You need to go back in there." I move toward him, turn him around, and push on his back.

"No."

"Hero, this is a huge award, and you weren't even done with your interview. Everyone in our industry is watching you right now: publishers, networks, and—"

"I don't care about any of that."

My eyes widen. "How can you not—?"

"None of it matters if I don't have you, Nora."

I open my mouth, ready to argue why he needs to go back in there, but of all the things I imagined he'd say, that wasn't it.

"Hero, this is your career. You have to go back. I don't want you to screw this up. We can talk later."

I grab his hand and start to drag him back to the convention hall.

"Nora, stop."

He stops dead in his tracks, and, using the hand holding mine, he twirls me around to face him. He spins me so fast that I have to rest my hands on his chest to steady myself.

"The only thing I'm worried about screwing up is what I have with you. The last two weeks without you have been the worst of my entire life."

With a finger under my chin, he forces me to look at him. How can someone's eyes say so much more than his lips? I practically melt under their watch.

"Mine too."

"Then why are we not together?"

"I …"

People start to file out of the room, slowly coming to a stop when they see us.

"This isn't the right time, Hero. You have to go back and accept that award."

He shakes his head. "Not without you. I want you more than that award. I want you more than my books or any opportunity that could come with accepting this award. None of it means anything if you aren't by my side. I'm in love with you, Nora. Short of a marriage proposal, I'm not so sure how else I can say it to make you understand. But hell, I'll keep trying till I figure it out."

My heart hammers in my chest.

I want you more than my books or any opportunity that could come with accepting this award.

But he's come too far to stop here. I won't be the one who stops him.

I grab his hand and jerk him behind me.

"Nora, I—"

"We are going back in that room, Hero. You are going to finish your interview and get that award; do you hear me?"

"Nora—"

I stop to face him. This man is relentless.

"And when you are done, I will be right there waiting for you. I will *always* be right there waiting for you."

His lips tug into a smile.

"Does this mean what I think it means?" he asks, stalling once again.

"Oh my god, yes. I love you too. Go. Get. That. Award."

Instead of listening to me, he slinks his arms around my waist and lifts me high enough to bring our lips together. A roar of cheering and clapping surrounds us, but that doesn't stop him from kissing me more.

"People are watching," I say against his lips.

"Let them. This is the happiest moment of my life."

I smile and press my lips to his once more. "Mine too. But for real, can we go get this award so we get out of here and go somewhere … alone?"

"God, you're smart."

This time, it's Hero who leads me back to the room. Everyone in the room must have picked up on our vibes because the awards ceremony goes very quickly, and before we know it, we are in the elevator.

Alone.

"I'm so in love with you," Hero says, pressing my back into the wall. He hikes one of my legs up to his waist and presses his erection against me.

My body responds like an addict about to go insane if they don't get a fix right this second.

"I love you too, Hero."

The doors ding, opening to his floor.

We untangle ourselves from each other.

"What now?" I ask, looking up at him. I'm no fool; I know

what happens next tonight. I'm talking about the future, and he knows it.

I'm expecting some long, sappy answer, but instead, he winks at me.

I grin to match his.

I might not know exactly how our future is going to play out, but I do know this: of all the men in the world that I could spend it with, Hero Quinn is by far the right one.

EPILOGUE

ZANE

One Year Later

I like to think I'm a smart guy.

I have always made goals and crushed them. I've always been good with my money. I've never been late on a payment. I'm honest and don't keep secrets. I'm loyal and trustworthy. I'm straightforward, and if I say something, I mean it. I've never done a single thing in my life that would result in karma or bad vibes of any kind, and yet the invitation I received in the mail from my brother says the complete opposite.

I scrub a hand down my face and take a breath.

I didn't even open the envelope. I know what it is, and I'm not fucking going.

"Dude, this is an engagement party, cheer up."

Beck takes the seat next to me and shakes my shoulder.

"Sorry."

He sips his water. "Something going on?"

I let out a long sigh. "Just family drama getting the best of me."

He nods. "Right. I uh, I got the invite today too."

I close my eyes and shake my head. Then I take a long pull from my beer.

"You should call him."

"Nope."

"You have to try."

"I really don't."

"It could help you move on. Who knows?" He nods toward Hero and Nora. "You could be the next to have an engagement party."

To this, I let out a fake laugh and then instantly stop to glare at him.

"This table looks like the most lively one here," Tobias says, the sarcasm in his voice thick as he pulls up a seat. Simon and Graham are right behind him.

"Who would have thought that Hero would be the first to settle down?" Beck says, watching our newly engaged friend pull his fiancée onto the dance floor. It's not a dancing kind of party, but there is music in the background and Hero is a true romantic at heart, so it's fitting.

"I'm happy for them," Tobias says. "They figured their shit out and are pushing through together. Our time will come."

That has got to be the sappiest thing I've ever heard him say out loud. In his books, sure, but not to our faces.

"Speaking of falling in love," I say, "who's that with Natalie?"

My friend's entire demeanor changes as he follows my gaze. He quickly looks away, shaking his head and focusing on his drink.

"That's Griffin, Natalie's new boyfriend."

"Boyfriend?" Beck, Simon, Graham, and I say in unison.

"Fuck, could you guys be any louder?" Tobias cringes and then takes a long pull from his beer.

"Since when does Natalie have a boyfriend? I'm not sure I've ever known her to have one," I say as we all focus on Tobias. He clearly isn't a fan of said boyfriend.

"Me either, but she's had one for about three months now."

Of course he knows the timeline. He's in love with her but won't admit it.

"And?" I keep the questions coming. I'm pretty invested in this new scenario.

"And," he sighs, "the guy seems pretty legit, and he really likes Natalie. He's good to her. She's happy. So, that's it."

"That's it?" Beck asks. "If he has a flaw, I'm sure you've found it. What is it?"

"You're all sure nosey right now."

"Spill," I say. "The sooner you do, the sooner this is over."

Plus, it's a great distraction from my life right now.

"I haven't found a flaw. He seems like a good guy. He even invites me to hang out with them. He has zero concerns about her friendship with me."

No one says a word.

"That's all I have. Let's focus on something else. Something like, oh look, Nora is trying to get Hero to sing at the karaoke machine."

The group chuckles.

"If anyone can get him to do that in front of a large audience, it's Nora. I'm glad he found her," Simon says.

Each of us quickly agrees.

"Bets on who's next?" Graham asks.

We all exchange glances with each other, and everyone points to Tobias.

"My time will come, but I don't think it will be anytime soon. But don't worry, guys, when it happens, it will be worth the wait."

One of us is always talking as if we're all searching for our own love story and we are just filling the time writing them till it happens. Maybe that's what we're doing, maybe it's not.

Which brings me back to my reality and the reason why I write romance stories instead of creating my own.

Falling in love … not for me.

THE END

Start reading Zane's book, Write About You, today in Kindle Unlimited!

Want a quick glimpse into Hero and Nora's happily ever after? Subscribe to my mailing list for an exclusive bonus epilogue!

MORE BOOKS BY JAMI ROGERS

The Black Alcove Series

Just One Kiss

Just One Night

Just One Touch

Just One Moment

Just One Spark

Just One Love

The Kiss Me Crazy Series

Kiss Me Crazy

Love is Crazy

I Want Crazy

The Evergreen Brothers Series

A Boyfriend by Christmas

The Summer Wedding Hoax

A Match by Christmas

The Lust or Bust Series

The Write One

Write About You

The Write Choice

Write That Down

More Than Write

Always Been Write

Standalone Novels

Love Money

Date in the Dark (A New Years Eve Novella)

ACKNOWLEDGMENTS

As usual, thank you to Julie, Jenny, Hang Le, and Dana for making this book happen. I love having you on my team. You make my dreams a reality with every single book and I wouldn't be where I am without you.

Thank you to the romance readers, all of you, even the ones who have just found me as a writer. The world you have created online when it comes to romance is more amazing than I could have ever imagined and I am honored to be a part of it.

Thank you to my husband Grant, and my daughter Brixon, for giving me a reason to stay disciplined and inspired with my writing. More books means more time with you and creating memories. I can't wait for our future together.

Cheers to the next book!

ABOUT THE AUTHOR

My name is Jami Rogers and I write new adult contemporary and adult contemporary romance novels. I *love* love and want to share my passion for happily ever afters with the world.

I was born in Wyoming and still live in the cowboy state with my husband, daughter, and two dogs. I like to read, write, run, watch movies/TV and spend time with my family. I'm horrible at returning phone calls and prefer to text, but still struggle to hit the little blue arrow to send a message once I'm finished typing my reply. My husband does 90% of the cooking in our house. Not because I'm busy – I'm just simply a bad cook.

Keep up with Jami by visiting her website www.authorjamirogers.com

or

Sign up for Jami's newsletter so you don't miss out on book news!

facebook.com/AuthorJamiRogers

instagram.com/jami_s_rogers

goodreads.com/jamirogers

bookbub.com/profile/jami-rogers

tiktok.com/@authorjamirogers